OTP

Adam Farber

Acknowledgment

I would like to give a special thanks to my friend Katie Hoffman and my mother Elvira Farber. Their support was greatly appreciated. My family, friends, and mentor's have helped make me the man I am today. A man known as Buddha said "Life is suffering."

I think it is more accurate to say that life is a struggle. That's all it is and ever will be. But there is hope so long as one person believes in it. Find passion and love in your life and share it with others. "There is only one true path. The one we create for ourselves." -Adam Farber

Table Of Contents

About the Author

Adam Farber, the author behind One True Path, wrote this mystical yet adventurous fiction story inspired by his personal experiences. He quotes, "Each character in this book is a true reflection of myself." initially, Adam wrote this book to overcome his own fears and insecurities and never planned to publish this book series. In the quest to find his true calling and meaning in life, Adam realized that writing had started to help him personally in his life. Adam chose to make this series public to assist others who have faced similar struggles. One True Path has just enough of a personal touch to give the reader a peek into his life. Adam believes that life is difficult and you need good people in your life. Adam would like to give a special thanks to his mother for her love and support. Also a special thank you goes out to Katie Hoffman, co-author of One True Path.

"This is something that I could not have done alone, Katie had put in a lot of effort for me and I appreciate it. One day I would love to see this as an animated film, I'd like for everyone to see what I've been seeing for years now."

Chapter 1: Our World

How could things have possibly gone so wrong? My mana had partially returned, but my body was slow to recover. My thoughts lingered on my last battle. Flashes of memories entered my mind, leaving me with a slight headache. I started to head over to the field where I fought the Necromancer. My legs still felt heavy and sore as I walked up a dirt mound. I wanted to see the battlefield again. I replayed the battle in my mind as I looked upon the destruction. I remember how exhausted I felt after the fight. My breathing was ragged, and my lungs felt like they were on the brink of collapse. My eyes scanned the battle-worn land; the trees that once stood high and mighty were scattered across the field. As I looked around, I saw a crater etched into the earth from my lightning attack.

It had filled up with muddy water from the storm I had created. To the side of the crater were lines of scorch marks from when I used my fire breath to attack the Necromancer.

I looked back at the city of Breon. The buildings weren't too severely damaged, but the streets had been flooded, and some of the power lines had been torn down due to the strong hurricane winds. I looked up at the sky and wondered, how did it come to this? We had everything: a healthy, peaceful world.

For thirty-five years, our people struggled with underdeveloped infrastructure, famine, overpopulation, political unrest between nations, and economic strife. Countries worldwide agreed to come together so that we could stabilize our world before it was too late. We had to stop the financial collapse and political corruption. We could not succeed without a leader. We needed a capable person who would assume a Neotaric position, someone who could unite us in working for a better future.

The best way to fairly decide who should take this vital role was to hold an election. We nominated three candidates for the Neotaric position: Robert Farvir, Liz Sharron, and Chris Benedict. These candidates were representatives of nations across the globe, and everyone was ready to listen to them. Robert Farvir explained that he had a plan to help set the world back on track. He said it wouldn't be easy, but he believed that as long as we stick together, the world could become a truly united nation.

It didn't matter how difficult it was or how long it took. We had the power to achieve a peaceful world. People believed in Robert's words and started to feel hopeful, but the other two candidates had different opinions. Lizz Sharon claimed that Robert was making empty promises. Lizz called herself a realist and said she would allocate funds to specific programs that would boost the economy.

On the other hand, Chris Benedict promised to end child hunger and create more jobs. Neither of them gave a clear explanation of how this was going to help the entire world. We had heard of these promises from the same politicians that got us into this mess. Chris and Lizz tried to convince the world that Robert's plan could never work, but Robert was resilient. He didn't acknowledge the other candidates and remained adamant about his plan. He stuck to his beliefs and hoped that we could overcome this crisis. He clarified that he planned to stop the ongoing wars and disband the major armies across the globe. We could utilize the extra money from the military budget to strengthen educational programs. Under Robert's command, a single language was to be taught worldwide, and a universal banking system would be established. Robert claimed he would create a Currency ID card that would confiscate the power from families who have monopolized the economy.

We listened intently to Robert's ideas, and people were enamored by his speeches. Robert Farvir became famous for his quote,

"There is only one true path.

The one we create for ourselves."

His words resonated with people from every nation. This was when everyone knew he would become our first Neotaric leader.

Robert followed through with his promises.

Soon, his words became a reality. He set his plan in motion and watched the world begin to heal. But after ten years, he decided to resign. To fill his position, a new Neotaric was elected. A man named Evan Markhill was someone who could uphold Robert's legacy. For the next twenty-six years, he saw a new optimistic future grow. Robert passed away in 2107, when he was 71 years old, due to a heart attack. Around the time he died, something happened that changed our world forever. A group of people called the Monks of Soul Run discovered magic in the land of Voth.

The Monks of Soul Run found what had been missing for more than a millennia. There were mysteries about our own creation, who we were, and where we came from. There were also unexplainable monuments on the planet that we couldn't replicate in this modern era.

The monks believed we may have been more advanced in the past before ancient Mesopotamia. One of them then went down to a local village and told the villagers that magic was real and that they wished to share their knowledge with the world. Word spread, and a group of reporters interviewed the monks at the temple to see for themselves. Once the reporters reached the temple, they saw some monks meditating in the courtyard, but a mind-boggling sight greeted them. One of the monks was flying above the temple, and another was repairing the temple with Earth Magic.

He used the stones from the courtyard to patch a hole in the wall. One of the reporters was skeptical and went over to the wall that was being repaired. He placed his hands on the stones and started inspecting the damage. The monk who was repairing the wall saw that the reporter was curious about his magic and said,

"Your eyes do not deceive you. This magic is real."

The reporter couldn't explain what he saw, so he turned to his film crew to ensure they captured this on video. Their footage went worldwide, but many people claimed it was fake. Some skeptical groups visited the temple to see if the footage was authentic. The general public didn't believe that magic was real, but the few that did were okay with people who could control the elements.

For twenty years, the monks helped people understand and Wield Magic. A young man wanted to learn about Elemental Magic from the monks. He ventured out to the Land of Voth to see it for himself. He was excited to train with the Monks of Soul Run, but when he arrived at the temple, it was deserted.

He saw signs of struggle all over the temple grounds, so he went to a nearby village and told the villagers what he saw.

The authorities started an investigation and sent out a forensics team. However, they couldn't reach any conclusions about the incident.

After the monk's disappearance, people began to fear magic. A woman running for Congress proposed an investigation into magic, but her pleas fell on deaf ears, and magic continued to get out of hand. Many people began to suffer from those who could use magic.

This same young woman ran for Congress again. She blamed the government for being unprepared because they did not listen to her. The public agreed with her and voted her into government. A new agency, the Investigation of New Magic (INM), was created.

A year after the initiation of the INM, rumors spread that a Necromancer killed an elite squad of INM agents. The citizens who heard about this demanded more protection. Unfortunately, things took a turn for the worse.

A man named Kash Johnson had the magic ability to control electronics. He created a computer virus and hacked the INM database.

The organization lost its drone missiles and recorded video footage. Without these surveillance devices, they couldn't find Johnson or the Necromancer.

Recently, a young man named Light had begun attacking INM agents in Breon.

Chapter 2: Unknown Son

I could sense someone behind me. I tried to ignore it because I was still wrapped up in my thoughts, but their presence was persistent. I heard a voice behind me, "Excuse me, sir. I need your help."

I tried to ignore his voice, hoping he would get the hint and leave me alone, but I could still sense he was there. He wasn't budging, he continued in his shakey voice.

"You're Ben Cardovic, right? People say that you fought the Necromancer."

His words finally caught my attention. How did he know my name? I continued to look forward, but my interest had peaked.

"Yeah. What of it?" I spat.

He replied, "I need to see Aaron."

That name made me stop in my tracks. I finally looked back at this kid. He looked exactly how he sounded. Small and scrawny. I could go as far as to say that a hard gush of wind was enough to blow him away. His dark hair was short and curly. It also looked like a mess due to the wind. I stopped to scan him from head to toe and asked, "What's your name?"

He replied eagerly, "It's Alex, sir."

This kid got me curious. So, I asked, "Why are you looking for Aaron?"

Alex replied, "My mother told me I needed to find my father. She's traveling with my grandma, and they won't be here for a few more days."

His reply caught me off guard. I had seen and experienced Aaron's memories. I thought I knew him inside out. I know his whole life, and

Aaron has no son, so I continued my interrogation, "Your father? Aaron doesn't have any kids. What's your mother's name?"

"Irelia," he replied worriedly.

Then it hit me. Irelia's face flashed in my mind. It was hard to forget her. She has a beautiful face with big prominent features. Her blonde hair framed her face perfectly, and her eyes could easily capture the heart of any man who laid eyes upon her. She was an enchantress in more ways than one. I began to wonder to myself, "The Enchantress? Is it possible? I have seen Aaron's memories. Is he truly unaware that he has a son?"

"Sir, I need to see him," his tone was now pleading.

"Let me get this straight. You are Aaron's son, and you came to ask me where to find him?" I asked.

"I have already asked everyone in Breon, and no one knows how to get to him, but they all mentioned you," he continued.

"Well, Alex, the short answer is that he's not here," I replied in a matter-of-fact tone.

"What? Where did he go?"

"The last time I saw Aaron, he told me he needed to find answers, and then he walked into some odd portal and disappeared. I haven't seen him since." I paused for a minute, gauging the young boy's expression before me.

"I've got a question for you, Alex. What do you know about your father?"

"I don't know anything about him. All my mother said was that my father was a remarkable person and a good man. She also told me he couldn't stay with us."

"What do you know about me?" I asked.

"I know that you're in the INM," he replied swiftly.

I started getting lost in my thoughts again. I ran a hand through my dull blonde hair and released a long sigh. Something about this kid made me want to keep him around.

"I think we can help each other out, Alex."

He looked up curiously, "How could I help you?"

"I have been working to stop criminals from misusing their magic for the past few years. Now that I've seen your father's memories, I've begun to question myself. I need you to look through my memories as well as your father's. I see two different versions of the same story; both cannot be correct," I explained.

Alex looked at me curiously. It seemed like he was thinking over my proposition. I waited patiently for his reply. A few moments later, he said, "I will help you."

I started second-guessing myself. Is this a good idea?

Should I be showing a kid all of my memories? He would experience so much pain, suffering, and loss.

So I tried to warn him, "Look, Alex, my life has not been easy. Your father's story is devastating, and I am a villain in it."

Alex looked determined as he said, "I will see this to the end. I came to find my father, and that's what I'll do."

Strange enough, his determination calmed me.

"Come, Alex, sit next to me."

I placed a hand on Alex's shoulder and began transferring some of my memories to him.

"Alex, I need you to steady your breathing and close your eyes." Alex started to see my memories enter his mind

"Ben, I keep seeing all these images of a mountain. It's so cold," he stuttered. "Those images are of my home. That mountain is called

Covenhiem. It's where I grew up." I explained.

Chapter 3: Covenhiem

My earliest memories were of a cabin located at the edge of a forested area by Covenhiem. It was known as one of the most dangerous places on the planet. It was considered inhospitable for humans, and the only person who lived anywhere near the mountain was my grandmother, Leela.

Grandma knew which parts of the mountain were safe. You might wonder what made Covenhiem so dangerous. It was the climate around the mountain which would change drastically and without warning. The weather could switch from scorching hot days to intense thunderstorms or heavy snowfall with strong winds in a matter of hours.

Different environments surrounded the mountain. To the west of the mountain was a desert area where scorpions and snakes roamed about freely. The South had a tropical jungle region with leopards, lizards, spiders, and other smaller mammals. Further south was a forested area inhabited by deer, rabbits, bears, and a pack of wolves that lived in caves between the desert and forest area. The east region was a swamp infested with alligators, insects, and fish. The north region had a rocky terrain that led to a lake.

It was lonely on the mountain. It was just grandma and me, after all. I had no other family. I had always wondered why. I don't remember my mother or father or if I even had any siblings.

When I turned six, I was able to comprehend the world around me. I loved going outside and exploring the different regions around Covenhiem. I would venture out every day to a different region. I liked to sit and listen to the different sounds of nature. I could hear the breath of the wind and feel the very aura of the earth.

After exploring and connecting to each of the regions around the mountain, I was able to sense everything around me. I felt bound to the mountain and rooted to the very land beneath me. I started to spend more time around the mountain than I did at the cabin.

But I would always check in on Grandma to ensure she was okay. I would occasionally bring her some wood or fruit when I explored the forested region.

One day, when I went to drop off some supplies I had gathered, I searched around the whole cabin but couldn't find Grandma.

I noticed some things missing from the cabin, so I thought maybe she had gone to town. I waited for her, but she never came back. I was only nine years old when she disappeared. I continued to live by the mountain because it was the only place I could call home. I vividly recall the day I was loitering around the mountain and saw a large plateau halfway up the mountain. I climbed up and took a look around.

I found a cave at the end of the plateau. It was kind of cold, but I felt safe up there. There weren't any animals, insects, birds, or bats in sight. The area was completely deserted, so I made it my new home.

One day, I went to check on some traps I had placed out in the woods. As I was looking around, I saw a small wolf wandering the forest floor. I kept my distance because the wolves, like the leopards, were dangerous. I studied the wolf and looked around for its pack, but it was alone.

I watched as it whined and wandered around the forest's flower beds. Its small and sad demeanor reminded me of myself, lost and alone. I watched over it from a distance. The poor thing was struggling. In my heart, I was rooting for it. I wanted it to find its pack. I think it was the first time the wolf pup was alone. I put some rabbit meat near it, but a hawk flew down and grabbed it before the wolf could get to it. I watched as the wolf pup drank from a muddy puddle.

Somewhere deep inside, I saw myself in the pup. The wolf layed down and began whimpering and crying. I told myself that I would take care of it myself. But then I heard a howl, and the pup's ears perked up. The rest of its pack had arrived and found the puppy. A wolf picked it up in her mouth and started to carry the pup away. I was happy for him because if the pup had gotten injured or sick, he would have no one to look after him.

Then it hit me. What if I got hurt or sick? Even the stranded wolf pup had a family. I returned to the cabin time after time in hopes that Grandma would return. Eventually, I lost hope. I accepted that she may never come back.

One day, while I was at the cabin, I started to look through some old newspapers left on the kitchen table. A section of the paper talked about an INM official who went missing. It seemed like everyone was mad at him.

Another section of the article talked about the Monks of Soul Run. The title read "**What Are We?**" and it caught my attention, so I continued to read about how the monks discovered magic. I got so excited reading about it that I decided to teach myself magic.

One day, as I was snacking on some fruit and mushrooms, I noticed the sky started darkening. I quickly checked my traps and ran back to the cave at the plateau.

As soon as I got to the cave, I felt the storm clouds rumbling. I peeked outside the cave as rain and thunder clapped overhead. Bolts of lightning tore apart the sky, and I could feel the electricity in the air. I could sense a strong energy surging directly above the cave. Suddenly, a flash of light struck the entrance of the cave.

My soul energy began to rise as a part of the cave collapsed from the intense lightning strike. I could feel this energy surging through my body, synchronizing with the lightning outside the cave. I stood up and gathered the energy in my fingertips. My hands trembled with bits of electricity dancing around my fingertips. With a flick of my hands, lightning burst forward, striking some dead wood at the corner of the cave.

The wood burst into flames and lit up the entire cave. I ran up to the fire and warmed my hands. It was so cold, and I was shivering all over.

I looked at my hands, intrigued, and then glanced over at the fire. I layed next to the flames and waited for the storm to pass. I had passed out and awoke to the fire crackling to its end. I started blowing on the fire to keep it burning, but the flame was getting smaller. I began to harmonize my breathing with the fire.

With one last breath, I realized that I was breathing fire. Once my fire was secure, I looked around and assessed the damage the cave had taken.

I felt a breeze coming from above me. I looked up and saw a hole blowing cold air into the cave. No wonder my fire was getting smaller. I dug my feet into the earth and placed my hands on the rocky cave wall. I could feel the earth pressing against the palms of my hands. I focused my soul energy on the cave walls next to the hole and began moving my hands closer to the center of the opening. The earth started to move with my hands, and I was able to seal the hole with the earth.

It was at that moment that I started to feel drained. I realized that I used too much of my energy. I laid back down next to the fire and fell asleep. The next time I awoke, it was around noon, and it was hot outside with no clouds in sight. I was still exhausted from the night before, but I made my way down to a small river about a mile from the cave.

I knelt beside the river and cupped my hands into the cold water. I drank a few handfuls and layed next to the river. I was in a daze. My mind was feeling a bit numb. What I didn't realize was that my hand was still in the water.

I could feel the water swirling around my fingers.

I poured my soul energy into the water. I feel the current moving and flowing. Before I knew it, I was speeding up the current, slowing it down, and I even made the river stand still. When I stopped the current, I could sense something moving in the water. In one quick motion, I quickly grabbed what was moving in the river, and when I pulled my hand out, I was holding a salmon. I made a small fire and relaxed in the shade till my food had finished cooking.

I started to feel a little better after eating something. Night came, and I snacked on some fruits that I had kept in the cave. I began to think of all the abilities that I had learned. Lightning, fire, earth, and water.

I wondered if it was possible to fly, though. Finally, an idea came to mind. I went down by the river and dug out a deep pit using Earth Magic. Then, using Water Magic, I diverted water from the river to fill the pit.

Lastly, I focused all my power and created a large rock standing fifty-five feet tall at the edge of the pit. I let myself recover over a couple of days before testing my theory. The general idea was to manipulate the wind around me while I fell.

Once I got over my fear of heights, I began to jump. Over the course of weeks, I had started to make some progress. I was infusing my soul energy into the air around me. Two months later, I could use some low-level Wind Magic.

It wasn't till month four that I flew for the first time. Since then, I started to fly as much as I could, not because it was convenient but because of how much fun it was.

I quickly learned that it was cold every time I took flight. I remember learning how to breathe fire so that I could stay warm. I wondered if there was a way I could keep myself warm internally with Fire Magic.

I started to use breathing exercises to try to heat up my body. With every breath, I began to let out light streams of fire.

I could feel my whole body starting to heat up. I took in a deep breath, raised my soul energy, and increased my body temperature even further.

I turned my body into a furnace; I watched as wisps of flames climbed off my body. The heat didn't hurt. In fact, it felt empowering. I jumped into the air and no longer felt the cold.

Chapter 4: The Outside World

Alex's voice broke me out of my trance.

"Hey Ben, sorry to interrupt, but how long did

you live on Covenhiem?" Grandma disappeared when I was nine, so I think I stayed in Covenhiem for almost ten years. I didn't start venturing out until I was nineteen. I slipped back into my trance and started to show Alex my memories.

I decided I didn't want to be alone anymore. I made the decision to go back to the cabin one last time. I needed to find modern clothes before heading to Ridgestone, the nearest city to Covenhiem. I looked around the cabin, reminiscing about my time with grandma.

I ended up in my grandmother's room. Now that I think about it, I don't recall ever being in her room. I was checking her closet when I found some men's clothes. They were a bit big on me, but it was the only thing I could wear.

I wondered why Leela had men's clothes in her closet. When I turned around to look at myself in the mirror, I saw a picture of Leela in a wedding dress with a man. She must have been married at some point, I thought. Oddly, she never spoke about him; he must have passed away when he was young. I found some jeans, a belt, and a red T-shirt that was slightly too oversized for me. Finally, I was ready to leave for Ridgestone.

I approached the city's edge and saw a man walking around in a daze. I was excited because this was the first person I had seen in years, but when I got a closer look, I realized he seemed tired and worn out. I asked if he was okay and introduced myself, but he just stood there. I asked him what he was doing. He said that he was supposed to go to the house to get new orders. I couldn't help but notice the bruises he had.

I brought him to my home on Covenhiem and laid him down in the cave. I checked his pockets to see if I could find any information on him. I thought it was strange that he didn't even have a Currency ID Card. I knew it was odd because even I had one. It was getting late, so I lit a fire to warm the cave and let him rest. The next day, I made him some food and got him some water. I watched over him to monitor his recovery. He stayed in that dazed and confused state for a few days.

When he finally started to come back to his senses, he spoke in a light and hoarse voice, "It's quiet now. I haven't heard the voices in a while."

The sudden sound rattled me, but I quickly recovered and asked, "Oh, you're up. So, tell me, why are you acting so weird?"

The man took a moment and started to talk slowly, "Who are you?" I told him that my name was Ben, and I found him wandering the outskirts of Ridgestone.

"Thank you," he replied. His eyes started to tear up, and he let out a deep breath as he explained, "My name is Rick. I haven't felt like myself for a long time."

"Why did you decide to help a stranger like me?" he asked.

"You didn't look so good, and I wanted you to get better," I replied.

Suddenly, Rick's face hardened, and his tired expression turned serious. "There are these voices in my head that tell me what to do. If I don't do what they say, they get more intense. I get nightmares and see illusions."

He took another deep breath.

"The suffering became so great that I just chose to follow their orders." He uncomfortably shifted around and winced.

"They kept giving me orders, but it was better than being in constant pain. I knew what I was doing, but I couldn't bring myself to fight against it anymore," his face contorted into an expression of horror, "Oh god, my family...I haven't been home in weeks or shown up for work. My family probably thinks I abandoned them or that I died."

I felt terrible for Rick, and I got angry hearing about his family. I asked, "How did you get to the edge of the city?"

Rick explained that he had just finished some orders and was returning to the house where the Mind Manipulator resided.

"I was so tired and hungry that I accidentally went the wrong way and ended up at the edge of the city," Rick recalled. "Rick, do you remember where the Mind Manipulator lives?" I inquired.

Rick's face turned pale as he let out rushed words, "No, you don't understand. They know magic!"

I put my hands on his shoulders and told him that I knew magic as well, so there was nothing to worry about. Rick looked surprised, "You know magic?"

I told him that I knew Elemental Magic. Rick slowly looked around the room and noticed that the bed he was sleeping on was made of earth. He looked up and realized that the ceiling was rocky.

"Where exactly am I?" he questioned.

"You're at my home in Covenhiem," I replied.

"What!? That's the most dangerous mountain in the world. You're joking, right?" he guffawed.

I failed to answer him because I remembered something.

"Oh, man! I forgot to check the traps earlier. I'll be right back," I said.

As I walked outside the cave, Rick started to follow me. When he walked out, he was surprised to see a beautiful landscape, vibrant and full of life. Rick was in awe of the breathtaking view. He looked below the plateau towards the jungle area and spotted a leopard in a tree.

"I should probably stay here until you get back," he stated.

I smiled and flew down to check my traps. I returned about an hour later with some melons. The traps were empty, but I had found some non-poisonous snakes to eat.

Rick didn't seem too excited about them, and he let out a nervous laugh as he said, "Snakes... mmm, sounds good. You couldn't find any deer or boar or something?"

I smiled and told him that snakes tasted like chicken. While I started to cook the snakes, I asked Rick if there were others that were being used, like him. He was afraid for me because he didn't want me to risk my life or end up like him.

"Look, Ben. Shouldn't we tell the INM about the Mind Manipulator?" He asked.

I told him that the INM had not done anything about it yet, so I would have to do it myself. Rick guided me back to Ridgestone and pointed out the Mind Manipulator's house.

It looked just like a regular house in the suburbs. Rick stayed at the edge of the city and refused to get any closer.

As I crept up, I saw a woman walk towards a gate leading to the back of the house. She had the same defeated look that Rick had. I followed close behind her and saw a few more people zoned out, staring at me with a blank expression.

The woman started to go upstairs and walked into a room on the left. I stopped just outside of the door and peeked in to see what or who was there. Other than the woman, there were three guys. Two of them were bulky and stood next to a couch. The third was sitting on the couch, and he was wearing a business suit. His light brown hair was swept to the side, and his light beard framed his face to make it look sharp. He was giving the woman orders.

The man on the couch seemed frustrated. He was annoyed that he had to be there, and he was angry because he had to look after these people. Suddenly, the man on the couch noticed me and looked me in the eye.

"Wait, I don't know you. How did I not hear you come in?!" He yelled at the other men, "Get him!"

The two men leaped forward and charged at me.

The man in the chair started to raise his energy, and I raised mine to prepare for a fight. Then I could hear them. The voices had entered my mind. They were all talking simultaneously, and I couldn't understand what they were saying. I wasn't able to focus at all. Then I felt a punch hit me in the abs.

I started piecing things together. The man on the couch must be the Mind Manipulator, and the two other guys were his henchmen. I looked up at the man who punched me, but all I could see were images of me dying on the floor. I couldn't feel any pain. I guessed that these might be the illusions I had heard about. I raised my energy as the voices started growing louder. They all shouted that I should die and that I should kill myself.

These voices could immobilize you. I thought of Rick and how he must have suffered from these abilities. I was being beaten while I lost my mind. My rage exploded, and my energy spiked more than ever before. I refused to die here. I refused to die like this.

I started creating hurricane winds in the room to push everything away from me. The voices changed from telling me to die to telling me to run away. In a fit of rage, I destroyed the room. When I opened my eyes, the room was empty. I looked out the window and saw that some of the people who were under the Mind Manipulator's control were running from the house.

I heard a vehicle start and saw the Mind Manipulator and his men drive off. My fists clenched, and I thought to myself, 'You're not getting away with this!'

I could see the Mind Manipulator turn his head to look back at me. I entered my empowered state and jumped through the window.

I started flying after them. I shot fire from my feet and hands to increase my speed. Once I got close enough to attack them, I started to shoot lightning bolts at their tires. The car swerved and struck a telephone pole.

The Mind Manipulator and one of his henchmen both got out of the car and started to run. One of his henchmen started to use his Illusion Magic, but I quickly flew down and grabbed him.

I dropped him mid-air, injuring but not killing him. Then I started hearing the voices again; I saw the mind manipulator using his telepathy to immobilize me and throw me off his trail. I continued to pursue him. Luckily, he tripped and landed on the ground. He knew this was the end for him, so he put his hands up in the air to surrender.

How could this man, who used others without empathy, feel fear? I shot a line of fire in front of him and landed on the ground. I walked through the fire and smoke.

I used Air Magic to increase my speed. I leaped forward and grabbed him by the neck. I shocked him till he lost consciousness. I found the last of his henchmen still passed out in the car.

I put the mind manipulator and his henchmen in their car. I attached some rope they had in the trunk to the front of the vehicle. I pulled their car to the nearest INM base in the area. I walked through the front door with the mind manipulator. "Hey, that's Jarvon Von Criegs!"

One of the men looked at the other and told him to call Gerard immediately. The man at the front desk, who recognized Jarvon, went over to check his injuries.

The INM agent then introduced himself. "My name's Taylor. What squad are you in?" he asked.

I told him that I wasn't part of the INM. He looked back at me with a confused look and said, "The commander of this base will be here shortly. We need you to stay here and answer some questions."

Ten minutes later, a large older man in his seventies approached me. Taylor introduced us.

"Ben, this is Major General Gerard. General, this is Benjamin Cardovic."

Gerard looked at the Mind Manipulator. He paused for a moment and then asked if he was dead or alive. Taylor told Gerard that he was alive, but he needed to be taken to the infirmary. Jarvon Criegs regained consciousness and looked up at him with a sneer and looked away. Gerard ordered Taylor to take Jarvon away.

Gerard walked up to me and extended a hand. He thanked me for bringing Jarvon, and then he asked me to follow him to his office. Once we got there, he told me he had some additional questions that he wanted to ask in private.

"Just to confirm, you are not in the INM, is that correct?" he asked.

I replied with a simple "Yeah, that's correct." Gerard gave me a curious look and asked, "Why did you go out of your way to capture Jarvon?"

I told him about Rick and what he had to go through.

"Rick told me that he wasn't the only one, so I felt like I had to do something," I explained.

"Do you know magic, Ben?" Gerard questioned.

I was honest and told him that I did.

"What kind of magic do you know?" I explained that I knew Elemental Magic like Lightning, Fire, Earth, Water, and Air. He raised an eyebrow and asked,

"Where do you live?"

"Well, I was living on in Covenhiem, but I decided to travel," I replied.

Gerard laughed and shook his head as he spoke, "It all makes sense now. Hey Ben, why not join the INM? We could use men like you."

I considered the offer and said, "Oh, I don't know."

Taylor had just entered Gerard's office to announce that Jarvon had been taken to the infirmary. Taylor had overheard the part of our conversation and spoke up, "Ben, Gerard is saying you could have a future here. The pay and the benefits are good as well," Gerard lowered his voice, "You would be able to travel as you want and help many people like Rick. There is an aptitude test this Friday at seven P.M. If you're interested, I will be there."

I was curious... "A test, huh? Sounds fun."

Gerard grinned as he spoke, "Excellent! I'll see you there, Ben."

Gerard escorted me back to the front desk and thanked me. We shook hands, and I left. I found Rick, who had reunited with his family.

It seemed like they were going through some hard times without him. I waited with them till the day of the aptitude test. I was very excited as I made my way to the INM training grounds in Palmdale. I saw people lined up in front of a table where a woman was giving out some paperwork. I told the woman I came for the aptitude test. She asked for my name, which I openly said, "Benjamin Cardovic."

The woman looked at her tablet and put her hand on her chin, puzzled.

"I see the name Ben, but there is no last name written here. There is a note saying that Gerard will be here at seven P.M. You still have a few hours until your turn. You can go ahead and get some food at our mess hall," she explained as she smiled and winked at me.

I thanked her and started to wander around the INM complex. I was exploring and looking at the buildings. I had never seen so many big, prominent buildings in my life.

People built all this, and they did it without magic? An INM agent was looking at me curiously and asked, "Excuse me, sir. What are you doing? You're not in uniform."

He seemed concerned, so I told him, "Oh, I'm just looking around."

He got very serious when he spoke next, "I need to see your Currency ID Card, and you need to tell me why you are here."

I got worried. I didn't understand what was happening, so I spoke nervously, "Gerard told me to come here for a test."

The man paused momentarily, then said, "If you're here for the aptitude test, you're not allowed in this area."

He was looking at my Currency ID card when a woman showed up. The man told the woman that my name was Ben Cardovic.

The woman was pretty. She had her hair tied in a bun. She cocked her head to the side and said, "Hey, I've heard that name. This was the guy who brought Jarvon to Gerard!"

The man remembered that he had heard about me as well. He introduced himself, "Sorry for getting all serious with you for a minute. My name's Tyler, and this is my co-worker Crystal."

Tyler and Crystal were talking about some rumors going around, but I wasn't interested in that kind of stuff. As I was walking away, I ran into an INM lieutenant named Dante.

Dante was a large man. When I ran into him, I was the one that got pushed back. I gave him a quick apology. He rolled his eyes and dismissed me.

Tyler and Crystal excitedly told him that I was the one who brought in Jarvon Criegs and that Gerard was coming to see my aptitude test.

Dante looked annoyed, but he started to size me up and study me. "Tch! You don't look so tough. I wonder what you would be?" he spat. Tyler and Crystal warned him not to get in a fight with me because my aptitude test was coming up.

Dante ignored them and asked me directly, "Let's see how good you are."

I told him, "I normally avoid fights, but I won't turn down a challenge. I'm down to fight after my aptitude test."

He looked surprised and said, "You're serious? I meant that as a joke. Most people try to avoid fighting me. All right, what time is your aptitude test?"

I told him that my test was at seven P.M. I was excited to fight against a real INM agent. Dante continued analyzing me like he was trying to figure something out.

"I'll see you at your test, Ben," Dante spoke as he continued to wander off toward another INM building. Tyler and Crystal got worried for me.

They said, "What are you doing? You can't just accept a fight after your aptitude test. Not only that, but you accepted a fight against Dante!?"

Crystal told me that Dante could transform people into animals. Tyler decided to speak up, "How are you supposed to fight a mage when you're a pug?"

I was getting frustrated with them, so I said, "I told Dante that I would be there and I won't back down."

I walked over to the barracks and continued to look around. I found some beds stacked on top of each other. I picked a spot and decided to take a nap. When I came to, it was already starting to get dark. I saw some INM agents walking by and asked when it would be seven P.M. They said it would be seven in ten minutes. I thanked them and started to head over to the training grounds. I was on my way when I heard, "Applicant one one seven, please come to the testing area."

I was excited and positive that they were calling my number. I quickly ran over and asked what I was supposed to do. The woman told me to go to the center of the testing area and wait for further instructions. As I was walking by, I spotted Dante on a bench by the test admin. To be honest, I had forgotten about the fight. I got so pumped up at the moment that I gave him a wicked smile.

As soon as I got to the center of the test area, I heard a familiar voice, "All right, Ben, show me what you got!"

Gerard had arrived and was eager to see what I could do. The test admin gave me a thumbs-up to demonstrate my powers. I began building up a large amount of energy and surged it through my body. I could see the test admin and Gerard talking about my energy levels. I intensified my energy and stomped on the ground while raising my hands. Three large pillars erupted from the ground. I launched myself into the air and flew around the pillars.

I levitated using Air Magic and then shot lightning bolts from my fingertips. The pillars exploded and broke apart. I took a deep breath and let out a large stream of fire, piercing the ground beneath me. I flew down and landed on my feet. As I was making my way toward Gerard, I saw a cold glass of water.

I used my Water Magic to pour it into my mouth.

I could hear Gerard yell out, "Damn, Ben, that was impressive! I like what you did with the water at the end there. By the way, that water was mine."

My lips curled as I tried to stifle my laugh. I thought to myself, "I hope I don't get marked off for this." Gerard took the tablet from the admin and then told her to get two glasses of water.

Gerard said that with my stats, I could start off as a captain in the INM. I would command my own unit and go on missions.

"I've got to file some paperwork. It will take some time to complete. You're free to stay at this base until then," Gerard said.

"All right, are we done? I've got some business to take care of," I claimed.

Gerard tilted his head as he spoke, "Don't start too much trouble. I'll let you know when we can proceed, Ben. I have some matters of my own to take care of."

Gerard walked off, and I turned my attention to Dante. His face had a look of shock on it, almost like something had spooked him. He shook his head from side to side and walked away. At the time, I was disappointed because I was looking forward to that fight. On the other hand, I wondered why he had backed off. Was it because he saw my magic or because he saw Gerard had a special interest in me?

Unexpectedly, I heard my stomach growl and realized that I hadn't eaten anything all day. I decided to make my way to the mess hall when I was dragged out of my memories by Alex, who politely interrupted, "You became a captain just like that?"

I clenched my teeth and winced. I momentarily stopped the memory transfer. "What's wrong, Ben? Why can't I see your memories anymore?" Alex asked. A look of confusion struck him.

I hesitated. I had pushed these memories to the back

of my mind. The next chapter in my life was darker than I cared to admit. Alex realized why I stopped sharing my memories, so he chimed in with words of confidence, "Hey Ben, I don't know what happened to you, but you got through it, so I'll be okay, too."

In my mind, I kept telling myself he wasn't ready. He had no clue about what I had seen or gone through, but I needed him. I took a deep breath before I continued, "Okay, Alex, let's push forward."

Chapter 5: The Necromancer

One week passed, and Gerard returned with the aptitude test results. I was eating in the mess hall when he approached me.

"Hey, Ben, how ya' holding up?"

I remember blurting out. "Have you tasted this bread stuff? It's amazing!" Growing up on that mountain, the one thing I had never had was bread.

Gerard chuckled and sighed. "Ben, we need to speak in private." When I walked into his office, he offered me a seat.

He then pulled out a tablet and started to bring up my file. "I spoke with other INM advisers about your file. I wanted to make you a captain so you could form your squad and go on missions. They disagreed, however."

I remember being annoyed and yelling out, "What! Why?"

Gerard seemed disappointed with this news as well. "To tell you the truth, they did make some good points. You may have scored high on the aptitude test, but you have never been in formal education. At this point, you have never lived in a civilized city. Now, I'm going to be straightforward with you. There's good news and bad news. The bad news is that I can't make you a captain right now. But the good news is that I can start you off as a first lieutenant on an existing squad." I listened to him quietly.

"First, you must complete some educational classes and then the physical training course. After a few missions with this squad, I can promote you to Captain. Honestly, this is just a formality. You will become a captain. With your power, I can see you doing great things. The other INM advisors want you to experience how the organization operates. We've already assigned you a team. I'll introduce you to them now." I followed Gerard to a large field with tons of training equipment. There was so much stuff I'd never seen before. I was able to spot some obstacle courses that reminded me of Covenhiem. I remember how I used to jump over fallen logs and climb trees; I got excited just recalling it. Something else caught my attention a moment later.

A guy started walking up to Gerard. He yelled," Is this my new lieutenant you talked about, Gerard?"

Gerard responded quickly," Yeah, this kid's got talent." He turned to me and said, "Ben, this is the captain""

I was so excited that I just wanted to look at some of the training stuff.

I interrupted them and asked," What's the fastest anyone has done the agility course?"

The Captain told me they didn't time it.

Gerard laughed. "Looks like you're going to have your hands full with this one, Captain. Get his EDU courses started.""

The captain nodded and told me to follow him.

I asked him what kind of training the EDU is. Now that I think back, I realize he was messing with me." Ben, the EDU is the most crucial training here. In fact, you're the only one that I've seen who has to take this course here. No one else has to do this." I was excited.

We walked to the end of the training grounds and headed toward a building at the end. My captain led me to a room with some desks and books.

"Ben, meet Professor Maeda." I walked over and introduced myself. "Captain told me you do some of the essential training I must undergo."

"Can you tell me what kind of training EDU is?" Maeda laughed and said, "The educational kind." I was so confused at that moment.

"Wait...What?" I asked.

Maeda continued, " Math, English, and some paperwork we must fill out."

I looked over to my captain, concerned.

He laughed at me again and said, "He's all yours, Professor. See ya later, Ben."

Initially disappointed, Maeda told me I could learn many exciting things. I admitted I wasn't precisely excited to learn Math and English. He asked me a question that caught me off guard.

"Is there something you want to learn?" At the moment, I didn't think there was anything I wanted to learn. I kind of just shrugged and shook my head.

"What about the origin of our world or where magic came from? How can we use these magical abilities?"

Instantly, my mind raced with what seemed like a million questions. He got me. "Ah, so you do like learning. I can teach you history as well."

He said, "We'll start with English. Soon, you're going to have questions, and you will need to hone your language skills to ask better questions."

About three weeks passed, and I was improving in English. Math was pretty simple to me.

We finished that in two weeks.

As a reward, he would tell me all the mysteries in the world. I was captivated by all of it. He brought out books, and we went over ancient and modern history. We had a lot of fun but went through it so fast that our time together ended quickly. I finished the subject in four days. I thanked Maeda for his help; he was right. I do love learning.

He brought out some paperwork and explained that I had to sign these documents to say I joined the INM officially. The next step was to start my recruit training. I woke up every day at Six A.M for the next three months. I had daily laps around the base and was given weights to bulk up.

On one of my morning jogs around the base, I spotted my captain and second lieutenant training. Then I saw it. My captain was shooting giant fireballs at a target. My second lieutenant was running through a complex agility course. I started getting really excited, thinking about how I would train with them and truly show them my abilities. Honestly, I thought their powers were impressive at first.

But I soon realized after a few days that they weren't improving. My Captain could only shoot fireballs, literally nothing else.

The size of the fireballs was always the same, and the speed at which he could fire them never increased. The second lieutenant rarely changed her agility course. She wasn't getting any faster. Like the Captain, they didn't know how to improve their power. I thought about this for a while. I wondered if Gerard had put me on a weak team on purpose. Was he punishing me?

These thoughts nagged away at my conscience. While I was working out, my anxiety got the better of me. I walked over to Professor Maeda's classroom. Maeda was surprised to see me. I could tell by how he sat back in his chair and touched his chin. Maeda was probably wondering why I had returned.

"Ben, you're looking stronger already."

I smiled. At least someone was impressed with my efforts.

"Thanks Professor, but I came because I need your help." Maeda was curious and asked, "What do you need help with?"

I told him about how I felt about the squad I was on. "Gerard hasn't contacted me in the last three months; I need to talk to him. Do you have his number?"

Maeda smiled. "This has been on your mind for a while, huh? I can give you his number, but you didn't get it from me."

He got a piece of paper and wrote the number down for me. Maeda told me to call him later in the afternoon. Gerard had a meeting that would take up most of his morning. I thanked him again and went on with the rest of my day. The next day, I waited 'till the late afternoon to give him a call. I walked over to the administration building in the INM base. I typed in Gerard's number on the phone in the office and waited. Finally, a woman answered, "This is the General's Office. How can I help you?" I asked if I could talk to Gerard.

She said, "State the reason for your call, your name, and rank." I thought she was joking, but she waited for me to answer.

"Look, can you just tell him Ben's calling?"

She seemed like she was getting mad at me. "Look, Ben, I still need to know the reason for your call and rank."

I could hear Gerard's voice in the background.

"Ben?"

He quickly told his secretary to transfer the call to him. Annoyed, his secretary did as she was told.

Shortly, I heard a click over the phone, and our lines connected.

"Hey Ben, What's the reason for the call?"

Still somewhat upset, I asked if we could meet up. Gerard asked what I wanted to talk to him about. I told him I would appreciate it if we could meet in person. He told me that he could meet, but not until after Wednesday. He was going to be busy this week.

Gerard told me he could come down on Thursday, which was fine.

Finally, Thursday came, and Gerard approached me while I was training. He studied me for a moment. "Ben, you look more muscular since last I saw you." I couldn't notice myself; I didn't feel any more stronger.

"Look, something has been bothering me recently, and I can't get it out of my head."

Gerard asked me, "What's on your mind?"

I sighed and asked, "Would you say the squad I am in is among the strongest?"

Gerard let out an "Oh" and started laughing.

"So that's what's been bothering you. I'll admit that this isn't one of our more robust units." He smiled at me before continuing, "Ben, please realize we put you on this squad because they needed a stronger individual. We wanted your strength to round out this squad."

I finally told Gerard that my squad's lack of power had let me down. Gerard heard me out patiently before saying, "Look, now that you have completed your training courses, your team is eligible for missions."

I started to feel better, knowing I was placed in this squad for a reason. I apologized and said, "Thank you for coming down, Gerard. I know that you have other important stuff to do."

He shook his head. "Ben, everything's going to be all right. I'll return in about a week with an assignment for your captain. We can get you up and ready for your first mission." I thanked him and headed back to the barracks.

I zoned out for a moment and started feeling anxious. Alex looked at me, concerned.

"Why did you stop sharing your memories?"

I started breathing heavily.

"Ben, what's wrong? You look sick," Alex started panicking. I tried to get my breathing under control.

"Ben! Talk to me. What's going on?" I knew what was to come next.

My first mission ...

I looked at Alex's face. He had no idea what he was about to endure. I began sharing my memories again.

Gerard returned six days later with an assignment for our captain. Our team was all lined up and ready to hear what our mission was.

Gerard began to go into detail about our mission. "All right, Ben, the rest of our INM operatives know this, but you will be hearing this for the first time. Tiers are what determine the type of job you will be fulfilling."

I was a little confused, but he explained that:

Tier 1 is guard duty

Tier 2 Patrol

Tier 3 Capture

Tier 4 Eliminate

Tier 5 classified

Each tier is ranked based on difficulty from D-S.

D-B rankings are considered medium-difficulty

B-A rankings are dangerous and hard

S ranking is the most challenging level; they are usually extremely dangerous for various reasons.

After Gerard explained the tier ranking system, he was ready to give us the mission. He brought out a file and handed it to our captain. He opened it and read: "INM squad 118, your assignment is Tier 3 ranked B. Target the Necromancer of Eldrich Crypt."

I remember feeling relieved that it was a capture mission with medium-level difficulty. Gerard looked over at me.

"This Mission will not be easy. Our last INM squad failed this mission," he warned us.

Our second lieutenant spoke up, "Wait? they died?" Gerard looked over at her, annoyed. "They failed to capture the target..."

He then motioned to our captain to continue reading the notes for our mission. Intel passed to us from other teams who have failed. Our captain read, "Low visibility due to constant fog and an unknown number of assailants in this graveyard." Gerard gave our captain the coordinates

"Your mission begins upon arrival. We have prepared some vehicles on the west wing."

It was still light outside, but our second lieutenant seemed worried and anxious.

"Why does it have to be a cemetery? I'm getting the creeps..."

Honestly, the second lieutenant was saying what we were all thinking.

We arrived at the entrance of a large iron gate. A plaque on the left of the gate read 'Eldrich Park.' We had a six-man squad: the three guys in our tech unit, the second lieutenant, myself, and my captain.

Our Captain began to give us our orders. "Tech Team, go set your equipment up at the lower level of that parking structure.

We need sensors and drones set up now. The second Lieutenant goes to the top of the parking structure and gets us a visual of the graveyard.

"Ben, follow me. We are going to check out the area around the administration building."

Everyone split up following the Captain's orders; we were all in position in about ten minutes. We got radio contact with our second lieutenant. "Hey everyone, I'm at the top of the parking structure. The sun will get blocked by some larger buildings behind the cemetery. Also, I spotted a fog rolling in from the center right-hand side of the cemetery. The fogs heading my way, and I will lose sight; I'll be regrouping with the Tech Team in five."

Our Captain contemplated what our next move would be. He gave our second lieutenant a fast "copy that" and then looked at me. "Ben, tell me your opinion on the situation." Something did strike me as odd.

"Did she say there was a fog rolling in?"

The captain gave me a curious "Yes, she did." I explained that it was barely sundown and it was not cold enough for a fog. "Also, I haven't sensed any wind in the last fifteen minutes; what's moving the fog?"

I think I worried him because he radioed the tech team later. "Hey, what's the ETA on those drones?" They radioed back that they had just finished setting up the sensors. The drones would be up momentarily. The captain also asked if the second lieutenant had met up with them yet. The tech team asked each other, and none had seen her yet. The captain said, " We'll give it a couple more minutes."

A few minutes went by, and I said the obvious. "Captain, she has increased agility. She should be there."

He nodded and radioed the second lieutenant. A long silence ensued. I could sense my Captain's anxiety growing. We were at the administration building. It looked abandoned. That's when I saw a fog eagerly creeping up on us.

"Sir, the fog is getting thicker." The Captain radioed the tech team.

But just like the second lieutenant, no one spoke up. I thought to myself, we needed to find our team.

"Captain, we should regroup with the others." He agreed. "Yeah, you're right. Let's go."

I saw some people entering the main gate; I motioned to him to look ahead. The Captain squinted to see better. "They're corpses! Ben, we have to get to the Humvee." He raised his hand and shot a fireball at a group of the undead, lighting them ablaze. It seemed to work, so I shot a steady stream of fire from my hands, trying to carve a path to the main gate. I looked around and saw more undeads closing in from our sides.

I turned behind us to see the undead blocking our last exit. I used Earth Magic to make a five-foot trench around us. It bought us some time, but we couldn't move fast enough.

"Captain, we have to get out of here now!" The moving corpses were climbing up the trenches. They would be within arm's reach in thirty seconds. It was too late. We were boxed in now. I stopped for a second and looked for any other alternative. Possibility after possibility went through my mind. There's no time and no way out.

I turned to my captain. "Captain, I'm sorry! There's nothing more I can do! I'm sorry..." I jumped in the air and flew out of reach of the undead.

My Captain looked up at me. "Ben! Don't leave me!" In a matter of moments, I saw him get swarmed. I watched in horror as I saw him cry for help. His screams of terror and desperation rattled me. A seething anger rose from me. "This can't be happening! How could you? They were decent people! You'll pay for this!" I was upset, but in my anger, I found focus. I reached out and connected with the fog using my mana. I could sense movement to the east of the admin building. I could feel a large amount of activity below the mist, circling a building.

I took a deep breath and blew the fog away, revealing a large mausoleum surrounded by undead. I gathered a large amount of mana and ripped open the earth.

It created large earthquakes, and I shook the earth till all movement in the area paused. I made a pit before the entrance to stop anything from getting in. I flew down and landed on some stairs. I opened a gate and walked inside the building. Parts of the building seemed to have collapsed when I created the earthquakes. As I ventured further in, I found the Necromancer half buried. It looked like the roof caved in over him.

The Necromancer was an older man. He looked over at me and muttered, "Stay away! No, wait! Help him! Help him! Could you help me? I thought he might have been speaking to someone else that was here. But I looked around and saw no one. Anger had built up within me, and I muttered, "He's crazy..."

I glared at him for a moment but had the clarity to remember that my mission was to capture him alive. The Necromancer reached out to me.

"Please! Please help!"

I hesitated. In truth, I didn't want to help him. He killed my team. But I had a mission to complete. I reached out to start removing some rubble when his extended hand fell. He had a blank expression on his face.

"No, no, no, I needed you alive! Don't tell me they died for nothing."

You see, Alex, this is one of the greatest regrets in my life. I failed my mission and my team.

Alex asked curiously, "What happened to your team? Did you ever find out?"

I did my investigation to find the truth. I grabbed the Necromancer's body. I figured they might still need it. On my way back, I saw an INM uniform ripped and bloodied. I didn't see his body, but that's where my captain was when I left.

I dropped off the Necromancer's body at the Humvee, then went to where the tech guys were setting up. There was nothing around the van; no blood, no corpses. I got excited and ran to open the vehicle door but saw death. The bodies of the three tech guys were lying there.

A few of the corpses being controlled must have forced their way in and attacked them. My heart started sinking, and my stomach was in knots. My eyes began to well up. I didn't see the body of our second lieutenant there. I went further into the parking structure to see if I could find her. I got to the middle level and noticed some blood on the floor. I followed the trail of blood till it led me to a corpse by an elevator. This corpse looked like one of the ones that the Necromancer had controlled. The elevator door wasn't opening like it usually would; the power seemed to have been cut off. I removed the panel before the elevator and searched for the power cable.

I put a small charge through it and opened the doors. I saw the second lieutenant in the corner with a nasty stab wound to the liver.

I yelled out, "Lieutenant, can you hear me?"

But she just sat there. I checked her pulse and realized none of them made it.

How did this happen? I thought to myself. The last we had heard from the second lieutenant, she said the fog was rolling in. I'm guessing she had just started heading down to the parking structure's middle levels when she got attacked. The fog must have surrounded her, and she probably couldn't see.

She would have just run around them otherwise. It looks like she got stabbed but made it to the elevator. She had shot the control panel on her side to lock the doors. This large group of the undead must have been the same one that attacked the tech team. After they killed the tech team, they came to the front gate and launched their assault on the Captain and me.

I went back and retrieved their bodies. I put them in the seats of the Humvee.

I used the Humvee's computer to route me to Gerard's base. When I arrived, he came out to greet me. He looked around to see if the Tech Van was still on its way. He then looked me in the eyes. "Ben, where's the rest of the team?"

I was silent. I was tired, more tired than I had ever been. Gerard saw the bodies in the seats and the horror I brought back.

"Let's talk in the debriefing room." We went to a small room with a mic and camera.

"Ben, I need to know what happened," he asked me. I told Gerard everything. I looked at Alex to see how he was handling this. The poor kid was crying and taking deep breaths. "What did Gerard say?"

Gerard buried his face into his hands. "Ben, this is on me. I put your team on this mission against my better judgment."

I told him what I was thinking of at that moment.

"I could have done more. I could have trained with my team and taught them how to improve their abilities. I could have got to know them better..."I blamed myself. Gerard tried to take the weight off of my heart.

"Don't blame yourself, Ben. This is my fault." I looked at him. "I don't even know their names..."

Gerard sighed. "I won't question you further; go get some rest."

I don't remember walking back to my bunk. My mind was numb. I lay down on my bed and tried to get some sleep.

But every time I closed my eyes, I replayed that night. I could see their faces. All these feelings just started to bubble up to the surface.

I could feel my *mana* rising, and I began to feel this pulling sensation in front of my chest, almost like I was drawing power from the universe. I no longer felt tired. It was a dark and gloomy night. I went back out to do laps around the base. Whenever I thought of the mission, I pushed myself to enter my 'empowered state.'

At this point, I became unaffected by the cold. I could shoot large fire blasts at a whim, even propel myself through the air like a rocket. Due to the high body temp, I couldn't be physically touched. The very ground I stood on burned after running four laps.

At the base, I began honing my abilities. I created three earth walls eight feet high and twelve feet wide to block intruders out.

I turned around and created a row of human-sized pillars lined up. I took one deep breath in and let out a long, fiery breath. This fire stream was about twenty feet long and burned the pillars. I flew up into the sky and raised my hands. I waved my hands back, charging them with Lightning Magic. Then I thrust them forward, firing multiple lighting streams from my hands. I destroyed the pillars and even enjoyed watching them explode. I didn't realize it, but I had been training for ten hours. Gerard came back to talk to me and walked up cautiously.

"I was told that you have been training all morning." I told him, "I've been training all night." Gerard asked me a simple question.

"Can't sleep?"

He hit on dead-on. I shook my head to answer his question.

"Look, Ben, I know what you went through was awful, but this is not the end. All we can do is learn from our mistakes, mine ... and yours." He held out his hand like he was going to hand me something.

I powered down and grabbed a piece of paper folded over. Gerard said, "You're being promoted to Captain."

I was in shock. "What? But I was only on one mission, and my whole team died. Why am I being promoted? I'm sorry, Gerard, I don't think I can do this."

He put his hand on my shoulder.

"Ben, I still believe in you. If you were to stop now, you truly would fail them. Think about it and let me know when you are ready."

I thought about what he said for a while. I opened the paper and saw five names on it.

Captain George Stevens

Second Lieutenant Paige Meadows

Tech Team Greg Chaddot

Tech Team Ron Burgens

Tech Team Jim Burgers

A wave of emotions hit me again. I shed tears and clenched my teeth. I remember saying, "I won't make the same mistakes again. I'll make things right ... I swear it." Then suddenly, the fatigue hit. I had been up for thirty-seven hours, been on one mission, and then went to train.

The moment I got back to bed, I passed out. I didn't dream that night. When I woke up, it was night. I looked at the clock and realized I had slept for twelve hours. I was still tired and sore but went to Gerard's office. "Gerard, I'm ready." He smiled with relief.

"You are making the right choice." I looked him in the eyes. "I made a promise. I won't let my team down again."

Gerard saw an eagerness within me. He saw I was ready to lead, prove myself, and command. He gave me a small stack of papers and told me it was a list of applicants I could pick to create my team. He also gave me an INM communicator so that he could message me directly.

Chapter 6: The New Recruits

Many of the INM agents had small rooms with just the basic necessities. Gerard told me I would be given a large private room now that I have become a captain.

The new room was extensive, with some nice appliances I knew I wouldn't use. I grabbed some water and headed over to the couch.

I sat down and started to look through the different applicant files. There were some with strange abilities and some with high scores on their aptitude tests. I had thought back to Captain Stevens and his team. I didn't like the fact that they weren't versatile. That they only had three members with magic, me included. I decided I wanted my whole team to be mages.

I was looking at their abilities when I noticed a woman who could control plant life. She was the only one in the INM who could, yet she had not been picked for two years. I wrote down her name and continued to search.

I saw a guy named Dylan Voss. His file said he learned Metal Magic at seven. Which, at the time, blew my mind because he had learned magic even younger than I had. At this moment, I knew what kind of team I wanted to create.

I wanted to learn more about the different elements and what they could teach me. I found another woman named Lauren Hills. She had the power to amplify Lightning Magic. I jotted her name down, too, and after some back and forth, I found my last member. He was on the previous page in the stack of papers I had looked through.

Jax Treck was an ice mage from a winter country. I saw some other extraordinary individuals with crazy powers, but these were the only ones I was genuinely interested in. I sent my request form to Gerard. He looked over the list and checked their abilities.

"Hmm... you chose other elemental mages?" he asked curiously.

I explained my reasoning, "I thought I could learn something from them, and maybe, in turn, they could learn something from me."

Gerard sat back in his chair and looked up at me.

"I'll send the request forms out. Your team will arrive in around one week."

I returned to my room to think of how I wanted to train my team. During that time, I continued to train.

While going through the obstacle course, A curious thought entered my mind. I got an idea but still had to ask for permission. I was notified that one of my team members had arrived early, and I went to greet and escort them around.

A vehicle pulled up and dropped this young woman off. I walked up and introduced myself. "Hi, I'm Ben; I'll be your captain starting now."

Sara was caught off-guard. She seemed nervous and shy.

"My name is Sara Harrison, sir. It's a pleasure to meet you." She was pretty and calm-mannered.

"So, if you're Sara, you must be the plant mage. I'm super curious to find out how you learned it. Go ahead, tell me about yourself." She nodded.

"Well, I grew up on a farm in Tuskin. We had all kinds of berries and veggies growing. Every season, we had delicious raspberries and blackberries."

She looked at me coyly before continuing, "I loved picking them up in the morning. I would wash them and put them in my yogurt. One day, I wanted to eat them, but they were out of season. I loved farming and eating what I planted. I placed my hand on the seeds and had this unconditional love flowing through me. I started to see the roots grow in my hands. I put them in the soils and continued developing them until they produced berries."

This was magic that I had never thought of, and it genuinely intrigued me.

"Wow! That's crazy. Can you show me?" I asked.

She nervously and slowly reached into her bag and pulled out some orange seeds. She gently placed the seeds in the dirt and smiled. At that moment, she seemed like some kind of angel. The orange grove began to grow around her 'till I could spot the oranges ripening. The sight left me in a state of wonder.

"Sara, that's amazing. Wow, I've never seen anything like that before."

I went ahead and started eating one of the oranges.

She went on to explain that one day when she was growing the other plants, her parents saw her and brought her to the INM. She continued her education while her file was passed around but never picked.

It boggled my mind because no one would choose this incredible power.

"Sara, you are unique, and this magic you discovered is incredible. Your magic has the power to make a difference."

Sara blushed and thought I was just being nice. She didn't realize I was being completely genuine. I had some other questions, and we talked while I brought her to my team's bunkhouse. The rooms were segregated, and Dylan and Jax would share a room.

Sarah and Lauren would share a room while I had a room to myself. I gave her instructions to go through an obstacle course that I would change up every day. Two days later, I got another notification that the rest of my team had arrived.

I greeted these three new members and brought them to our training grounds. I had us all introduce ourselves. I was first, and Sara followed. One young man spoke up after Sara. "My name's Dylan Voss. I discovered Metal Magic when I was seven."

A young woman with a fiery spirit yelled out, "My name is Lauren Hills. I learned how to hone my lightning powers when I was twelve."

Lastly, there was Jax. "Name's Jax Treck. I learned Ice Magic when I was sixteen."

After we all got to know each other's names, I took each of them aside so that I could ask more personal questions. I walked with Dylan and asked him, "Dylan, can

you tell me the first time you realized you could use Metal Magic?" He told me the INM had already asked this question before, but he didn't mind answering again.

"My father was an engineer, and my mother bought me a metal Kinect set so I could build things like my dad. I was trying to develop something tricky with it one day but found out I didn't have the right piece to finish my project. I reached out and started to envision the piece I needed in my mind. Suddenly, some pieces in my hand had transformed into what I saw in my mind. I was able to complete the structure. I showed my dad what I had created. He had a keen eye, so when he inspected it, he saw a piece inside that shouldn't exist. He asked me how I made the metal piece after I told him. He contacted the INM, and they continued my education up until now."

Dylan's story was similar to Sara's in some ways.

After a lap around the base, I asked Lauren to come accompany me. I asked her the same questions, mainly how she learned her power. Lauren told me she found out about her ability at a science fair. She created a device that could detect mana but realized she didn't have the necessary energy to power her device.

Lauren's anxiety grew when the judges were getting closer to her project. She began to panic and used her own mana unknowingly to increase the voltage inside the device. Her device started to buzz, sensing Lauren's mana being used.

A judge who was a well-known scientist asked to see what powered the machine. Lauren saw him do the calculations in his mind. He shook his head and told her that it wasn't possible. He notified an INM agent who was there, and the organization contacted her family.

Just like Sara and Dylan, she was sent to the INM to pursue her education. Next, I walked with Jax ... well, Jax was still a mystery.

He told me he didn't realize he was immune to the cold until he was sixteen. He grew up in a cold region and loved it there, always wanting to be outside and in the snow. He only recently figured out he could control the temp around him and even create ice. Jax was the only one I knew who wanted to join the INM and went on his own accord. Once I learned more about them, I had them put their bags away and rest.

The following day, I had each of them display their power to the rest of the group. After I saw their abilities, I showed them mine.

They were shocked to learn that I could use Lightning, Earth, Fire, Water, and Air. What really shocked them was that I could use multiple elements simultaneously.

I asked each of them individually to try and help me learn their power. I discovered Ice Magic from Jax, Enhanced Lightning Magic from Lauren, and Metal Magic from Dylan. Plant Magic was the only magic I found myself having a hard time with. I had to come to terms with the fact that I might never learn that one.

One thing I didn't expect was Lauren's comment, "It's probably for the best that you don't learn Plant Magic. I mean, what are you going to do, grow flowers for our enemies?"

I glared at her momentarily before speaking up, "Sara is unique, and her power is rare. No one else in the entire INM has had this power before."

Lauren realized her joke was not being taken lightly. She apologized, although it didn't seem sincere. I listed what I would teach my team to make them stronger.

First, I needed to teach Lauren to hit multiple targets with her Lightning Magic. So far, her Enhanced Lightning attacks have been simple and straightforward. Lauren and I taught Dylan Lightning Magic. I taught Sara Earth Magic, then showed Jax Water Magic. After a couple of months of training, they became more familiar with their new powers. However, none of them were really getting along. Dylan and Lauren constantly bickered. They treated Jax like an idiot and saw Sara as a burden.

Dylan was excited that he had finally joined an INM squad.

Finally, he could go on missions. During a lunch break, Dylan asked, "Captain, I heard you killed a Necromancer on your first mission. I just have to say It's an honor to be on your team. You have no idea what it means to me."

The recent past pained me greatly. Still, my response was a bit cold.

"You're right... you have no idea." I turned away and lay down on the grass. I could hear Dylan ask, "What's with him?"

Jax apparently had heard the truth. "You are correct, Dylan. He did kill a Necromancer on his first mission. But the mission was to bring the Necromancer in alive. Not only did the mission fail, but his entire team was killed."

Dylan let out an "Oh, shit! I didn't hear that."

I contacted Gerard to see if I could take my team to Covenhiem to train them there. Fifteen minutes later, he gave me the green light.

I gathered my team and told them that I had an announcement.

"Before we go on any missions, you must pass a test before I even recognize you as members of my team.

Dylan spoke up, "What kind of challenge will we be facing?"

My reply was direct, "Survival. You must live on Covenhiem for two months."

Lauren panicked and shouted, "That's the most dangerous mountain in the world!"

Dylan asked, " So when do we start?"

I turned to Dylan and told them, "We'll be leaving tomorrow morning." I told them I prepped some MRE supplies, toilet paper, pots, pans, and other essentials. It was going to be a two-hour drive to Covenhiem.

During the ride, I could feel myself getting excited. Home... I had thought of Covenhiem. Often, it felt like the whole area around the mountain was my domain. My mana was restless; I could feel it coursing through me.

When we arrived, I first saw the cabin where I grew up with Grandma. It made me smile. Those were fond memories for me.

I took my team through the forest towards the mountain. My group studied their surroundings; they had never seen nature in its purest state.

We had passed the forest and made it to the jungle region. We continued till we reached the base of the mountain. We hiked up until the trees were covered with snowfall.

I stopped and told them, "This is the spot."

We were at a high altitude where the air was thin, water was harder to find, and food was scarce.

I told them what made the mountain so dangerous: The weather around Covenhiem changes drastically and constantly.

Dylan seemed like he had a question. He was ignorant and a little arrogant.

"What's the point of the test if we all share the same powers as you?"

Jax interjected, "Dylan, You're incorrect on that assumption. No one on this team other than the captain knows fire or Wind Magic. Not only that, but our captain grew up here and discovered his powers here. Not to mention that we only have a fraction of his powers. He has the whole package."

Dylan thought on it for a moment before agreeing with Jax.

"If you can live here, I will acknowledge that you are worthy of my command. You have two months; your test starts now," I continued up the snowy mountain toward my cave above. They did not know it, but I had begun my own training. As they started their test, I sat in meditation.

I let my mana expand outwards into the elements. I could feel what was happening around the mountain. I could feel their warm breaths in the air, The wind pressing against trees and animals alike. I could feel my team's steps on the ground beneath them. My plan was to monitor them from a distance. I used Wind Magic to hear them from afar.

Dylan was the first to take control of the situation.

"Listen up, guys, we have to stick together," he said, trying to comfort the others.

Jax nervously pointed out that a storm was rolling down from the upper parts of the mountain.

"We need to find shelter now." Lauren looked to see if she could spot anything that could be used as shelter. After a quick look around, she came to the realization there was nothing out there but empty wilderness.

"We'll have to make a shelter," she declared. Dylan turned to Sara.

"Ben taught you Earth Magic, right? We need you to make a shelter for us."

Sara panicked. I knew she had never made anything this big from training with her.

"Earth Magic uses a lot of mana, Dylan. I would have to use all my mana to make it."

Sara pushed herself and was able to create a medium-sized cave but began breathing harder afterward. She had exhausted over half her mana with just one use of Earth Magic. The weather around them started to grow colder.

Dylan voiced that even if they found wood, it would be too damp and couldn't be used for firewood.

Dylan came up with an idea: "Jax, can you extract the moisture inside the wood?" Jax scoffed at Dylan, "Technically, yes, but I've never done that before."

Dylan told Jax the truth, "Look, Jax, if you can't do it, we have no fire, period." Lauren looked at Jax and said, "All we are asking is that you try."

Jax sighed. "We still need to get wood." Dylan gathered some cooking knives and made two axes from their combined metal.

Dylan shouted, "Lauren, stay with Sara; Jax, come with me."

The two began chopping away at a tree close to the shelter. The snow and icy wind were sapping Dylan of his strength. He tried a different tactic of changing the axes into a large saw. Finally, they were able to make some progress and get some wood. The storm was getting more robust, and the medium-sized cave barely gave any protection from the weather.

Jax sat down next to the pile of water-logged wood and concentrated. He focused intensely until he was able to extract the water from the wood.

Once they had dry wood, Lauren shot out some lightning and created a small fire for them. I was disappointed in their progress.

Sara used only half her energy and created a half-assed shelter. All Lauren did was zap some wood, and Dylan was not using his abilities to their fullest potential. Their fire wasn't helping them at all. It was too small.

This is sad; they cannot survive like this, I thought to myself. I flew down from my cave to give them proper guidance.

I stood before them and shouted, "Get out of the shelter!"

You don't know how to use your powers. I scolded them, "Sara! This won't do. Your team is counting on you to keep them safe."

She tried to explain herself, saying, "But I've never made a structure that big. It would drain all of my energy." I was upset... How could she see it like that?

"Sara, their lives are in your hands, and you gave it fifty percent." She looked back at her teammates and then back at me.

"Sara, please save their lives... raise your mana."

She was upset and crying. I might have been tough on her, but you give it your all when saving lives. She turned toward the shelter and began to lift up more earth. I gave her some advice on making shelters with Earth Magic.

"Make an enclosed structure with two vents. Make the entrance of the shelter the size of your biggest man."

I watched her struggling and yelled out, "Push, Sara, push!"

With the last of her strength, she stabilized and forged a bigger shelter. She fainted just as she had finished. I picked her up and placed her in their new sanctuary. I was proud. She really gave it her all. Even if she had failed, she knew she had given it everything.

I looked at what little wood they could gather and shook my head. "You need more wood. Jax, I'm impressed you were able to use an ability I didn't even teach you. If I recall, you don't feel the cold. Use your jacket to drag the wood into the shelter."

I told Dylan and Lauren to follow me to get more wood.

Lauren's eyes widened. "What do you expect me to do? Chop wood in a snowstorm?"

I stared at her coldly. "I expect you to use your head."

Dylan argued, "Ben, Lauren doesn't have the physical..." I interrupted, "Are you saying she can't do it because she's weak?"

They looked at each other and stood in silence.

"Now, follow me. We need to get more wood."

I walked over to where Dylan and Jax had started chopping.

"Dylan, use your Metal Magic to create a sharp disk.

I need you to spin the disk as fast as you can. Lauren, I need you to energize the disk with your enchanted Lightning Magic. The silver blade sparked and began cutting through the tree like butter.

Now, they started to get some decent-sized logs. Jax would take the wood and drag it back to the shelter, where he continued to remove the water.

After fifteen minutes, they had enough wood to last the night. They returned to their shelter and created a more extensive fire. Finally, they had a real chance to get some rest.

I went back to my own shelter up on the mountain. I created my own fire and got some sleep. When I awoke the next day, it was warm outside, but it was overcast, which made it humid.

I checked on my team and found them eating their MREs. They were still exhausted. Right around thirty-five percent of their normal mana remained. I let them rest and went to do my own training. I walked around the side of my cave and made a ditch. I gathered the overcast clouds filled with water and made them rain into the pit I had created. Just like that, I started a freshwater reservoir.

I hid out of sight and listened to what they were chatting about. I could overhear Lauren complaining about how the weather changed overnight. Then, it went from overcast to no clouds in sight.

Jax turned to Dylan, "What are we supposed to do now?"

Dylan shook his head and thought about it.

"We were told to live here."

Jax countered, "This is a survival challenge."

Dylan argued, "Surviving is what we're doing now, But that's not the same as living. Ben grew up on this mountain; he lived on it. We need to do more than just survive. Our captain had to adapt to the other weather conditions that battered this mountain."

Jax nodded in agreement but added, "The safest place we have is our shelter. It's not like we can just tunnel underground and roam around." Dylan realized that might actually be the answer.

"Jax, that's actually the solution. We'll tunnel around so we won't be exposed to the elements and can still move freely."

Dylan ran over to Sara and asked if it was possible to build a tunnel system using Earth Magic. I laughed behind a tree. Sara's jaw dropped when Dylan asked. She just used all of her mana and built a shelter just big enough for them. Now Dylan's asking her to create something even more significant.

Sara started calculating how far she could go if she tried to make a tunnel with Earth Magic.

"There's no way... I don't have that kind of mana."

Dylan asked, "If you gave it your all, how far could you get?" Sara answered, "Dylan, if I gave it everything I had, I would get about fifteen feet tops." He shook his head.

"Damn, that's not good enough. What if Lauren and I started tunneling? Could you prevent cave-ins?" Sara nodded. "Yeah, that's doable."

Dylan ran over and grabbed Lauren, and let her know the plan. Dylan then gathered all the metal they had and started to create a drill. He began to spin the drill while

Lauren used her Enhanced Lightning to empower it, just as they did when they cut wood with the metal disc.

Dylan started to dig underground, and Sara stood behind them, hardening the earth above the tunnel. She created pillars to strengthen the structural integrity of the tunnel.

Jax was behind Sara, removing excess dirt to clear the pathway. Honestly, I was impressed with their progress. They had figured out a way to maneuver around Covenhiem freely. I also noticed that they started to work together and argue less.

While they were taking a break, I approached them to tell them how proud I was. I invited them to come to my own cave to rest.

They walked into my cave and were amazed by what I had created. The fact that I did it all myself is what baffled them. I caught some deer down from the forest area and made them some food for the night. We laughed and bonded around a firepit. I liked their idea of a tunnel system and decided to work with them. I began helping them with the tunnels the following day. We continued to tunnel all throughout Covenhiem.

A tunnel led to different regions around Covenhiem. I even connected a tunnel to my cave halfway up the mountain. Sara and I created a large underground cavern that connected all the tunnels.

In this cavern, we had created a well and a water system to ensure we couldn't be flooded.

Sara started to draw a map of Covenhiem. She went to the forest and jungle areas and collected different fruits, veggies, and other plant life.

Dylan and Lauren created a bath inside the cavern with a metal bottom. Lauren could channel her Lightning Magic through the metal rods to heat the water.

Sara began to plant some of the seeds she got from the forest and jungle. We all watched as the plants sprung up. I couldn't help but wonder what a fantastic ability she had. She created an underground greenhouse. Sara herself made an area for them to thrive, even if it was underground.

Jax carved out some gutters that funneled water to the plants, and Sara also grew a sequoia tree that grew large and tall.

It popped out of the cavern and into the light. I opened a part of the ceiling so that it could continue to grow without hitting the roof. Finally, after three months of hard work, we completed our objective. We celebrated by eating fresh veggies and fruits from the garden. We sat around a fire and laughed together.

My team didn't just survive on Covenhiem, but they thrived here. None of them even complained that their challenge was extended past its original deadline. I stood up in front of the group and gave them my thoughts.

"Sara, if it hadn't been for you and your Plant Magic, your team would have had difficulty gathering food. You ran out of MREs last month."

Dylan stood up and looked at Sara. "Sara, I'm sorry; before this test started, I thought you were the weakest one in our group. Now I see that we relied on you the most out of anyone. We never would have made it this far without you." Sara blushed and smiled. Lauren and Jax got up and thanked her as well. Lauren also apologized that she belittled Sara earlier. This time, it was heartfelt and genuine.

Sara accepted their apologies graciously. I was proud of them; they came together as a team and became friends. I couldn't help but wonder if this is what having a family felt like.

I told them they had passed their test and I would be honored to have them on my team. I told them I had one last thing to do before we could leave. I gave the order to get some sleep. Tomorrow would be our last day at Covenhiem. Honestly, they were all disappointed; they became fond of this place and the lifestyle they created.

The following day, I journeyed to my cave before the rest of the team woke up. I went up to the cave wall above my bed and began to etch the names of my first team into stone. Dylan and Jax had poked their heads around the corner. I guess they followed me to see what I was up to.

Dylan straight up came out and said it.

"Ben, what are you doing?"

I told them the truth. "These are the names of the people in the last squad I was in. Jax, you were correct. They all died on that mission. I failed them but vowed I would never fail like that again."

There was a moment of silence before I walked to the cave entrance. Dylan and Jax tilted their heads, wondering why I wasn't heading back through the tunnel system.

I glanced over at them and said, "I'm going to help the girls get ready. I'll meet you down there."

I entered my empowered state and shot flames from my hands and feet. I rocketed down the mountain to where our cavern was below. When I landed, both Lauren and Sara stared at my empowered, fiery state.

"Let's start packing. We're leaving in one hour."

I powered down and started to help the girls pack our gear. When Dylan and Jax arrived, we were finally able to leave Covenhiem. Once we got back to base, everyone was tired, but they also missed living on Covenhiem together.

We all took showers, got some food, and went to bed. I got a message from Sara asking if we could talk in person. She stopped by my room to talk about it. I opened the door and invited her in.

Sara got me a glass of water and asked for me to take a seat.

"Ben, thank you personally for choosing me to be on your team. I had been waiting at that INM base for years without being selected. You were the first person to pick me; I felt scared, weak, and filled with self-doubt. You defended me. You called me rare and unique." She blushed.

"Not just my power but me. During that test on Covenhiem, you believed in me. That was the first time I had ever given my all. Now, I'm on a squad, respected, and depended on. Ben, you have changed who I am."

Sara wrapped her arms around me and held me. She leaned in and kissed me. It was the first kiss I'd ever received, and I stayed with her throughout the night. It seemed so serious. In some ways, it all felt like a dream. All I knew was that whatever it was, it was mutual.

I woke up early that morning to get ready in the waiting room. I put my pants on and walked out carrying my shirt and shoes. When I saw a door open down the hall, it was Lauren's door, but Dylan walked out with only his pants on, carrying his shirt and shoes. We looked at each other in awkward silence. Dylan spoke up, "Good morning, Captain."

I replied, "Good morning, lieutenant." He went back to his room where Jax was. I thought to myself, well, at least we're getting along. Late that afternoon, we met at the mess hall for lunch. While eating, I announced that I wanted to do more combat training.

After we ate, we headed over to the training grounds. I gave them all specific instructions on how to improve themselves.

Dylan learned not only how to use Lightning Magic but also how to empower his metal weapons without Lauren. Lauren was to focus on her agility.

Jax was able to turn water into ice, but what he needed to do was be able to freeze water at a much faster rate.

I trained Sara on how to create more efficient earth walls. I had her match every structure that I would create. Sara could use the roots of plants and trees to ensnare her targets or kill them if necessary.

Dylan's Metal Magic continued to advance and evolve. Lauren became fast, and her Enhanced Lightning Magic became powerful.

Jax mastered his Ice Magic but also vastly improved his Water Magic. During our training, we heard a familiar voice. Gerard had arrived and asked to see them demonstrate their powers.

Alex interrupted, "Hey Ben, I didn't notice before, but Gerard looks like my Grandpa, but he looks older here. Like, he looks a lot younger the last time I saw him." Now that I think about it, I did notice Gerard looking a bit younger. His grey hair darkened, and he lost some of his wrinkles. I didn't know what he was doing, but I didn't think much about it at the time.

Alex explained that he had only ever known him as "Grandpa" and didn't remember hearing his name. We both thought it was odd. Neither of us knew how Gerard started to look younger. Alex asked me to continue with what was going to happen next. He just wanted to point this out to me.

Gerard wanted to see my team's progress since our journey to Covenhiem. Gerard suggested a skirmish between me and my squad.

I told them to defend themselves against me. I started by shooting lightning bolts. Sara created an earth wall to protect them.

Dylan leaped out behind the wall and shot lightning bolts back at me. I dodged and moved back to create some distance. Dylan wore this metal armor that he could change into just about anything. He decided to dismantle it and create a metal net. Every time I fired a lightning bolt at him, he could catch it with the net, nullifying my attacks. I noticed that Dylan was looking behind me. I turned to see Lauren with an empowered lightning bolt. I flew up to make it harder for her to hit me. As expected, by flying around, she was unable to land an attack.

Sara used her Plant Magic and covered the area with plant life, giving them cover to hide behind. I shot a large stream of fire, burning the vegetation to ash. Jax had begun shooting icicles at me, which I quickly turned back into water. I could feel the air temperature getting lowered.

It forced me into my empowered form. I saw Sara lower the earth wall she had made.

As the earth wall dropped, I saw that Dylan had created a metal ballista, and Lauren was empowering the metal spike. It was an impressive display of power. As they were just about to fire, I caused a quick earthquake, causing the ballista to misfire.

I shouted, "Enough! The demonstration is over."

Gerard was shocked by how powerful my squad had become. He chuckled, "They almost had you."

I grinned, "Not a chance." I walked over to my team.

"You guys did great. I'm proud of all of you. However, didn't I tell you to defend?"

Dylan said, "The best defense is a good offense."

Chapter 7: Tough Decisions

Gerard messaged me that my squad had its first mission and to meet in the operations room at noon.

I sent out a group message telling my squad we had been assigned a mission. I explained that we would find out the details from Gerard. The minute we walked in, Gerard handed me a thick file. I pulled out the first paper in the file and began to read. "T4-A ranked mission. The target is a human smuggling ring. Our intel indicates that this group deals with human trafficking. These human traffickers have kidnapped well over a thousand people, primarily women and children. They have been active for twelve years now. The HSR has access to advanced weaponry. Their leader's name is Quinn Hails."

I looked at my team and then continued, "She will be at a port in Varrok tonight at eleven thirty." I had this feeling of anxiety creeping in. I couldn't help but think of my first mission. Gerard cut in, "This mission is simple. They are to be eliminated." Dylan asked for details on what kind of advanced weaponry they had.

I flipped past a few pages and read, "The weapons they use shoot energy rays from modified guns. The power source is unknown. It also says here that most of them have increased speed. There are no details as to how or why, though."

Gerard told me there was more information on the location further down the page. "It looks like the gang will be meeting at a warehouse. Not only Quinn Hails but also other high-level members of the HSR will be there. If we strike now, their entire human smuggling ring will fall apart. Dylan was looking at a map of the area."

Dylan gave me some valuable information: "Captain, many of these HSR members have increased agility. However, we can block off the exits and trap them in the courtyard."

I took a look at the map myself and saw what Dylan saw. A plan started to form in my mind.

"Dylan is right. If we trap them, then their speed won't matter. Also, their weapons are still made of metal-based substances. We can still use Metal Magic to disarm them. My plan is to win with overwhelming power. This could be tricky, but I believe we can pull it off. Okay, here's the plan, Sara. I need you to create earth walls to block the roads. Jax, I need you to sneak into the back of the warehouse and begin lowering the temperature inside. We need to draw them out. Lauren, go with Jax and short-circuit the breakers; let's turn off their power and leave in the dark. Dylan, I need you to sit on the roof above the front entrance. When they enter the courtyard, seal the metal doors shut and remove their weapons."

Dylan asked, "What then? Do we attack as a team?" I wanted to test a new ability. I told Dylan, "No. I will engage the enemy alone. I need you to get out of range when you see the signal."

Dylan questioned, "What kind of signal?" I told him, "You can't miss it." Dylan shrugged and shook his head, then asked, "Is there any kind of weapons or technology we should bring?"

My response was quick, "The world is our weapon. Once we disarm them, I will have a massive advantage."

Now that everyone knew the plan, we began preparing ourselves and loaded up the Humvee. We set off on our mission towards the port of Varrock.

As we got closer, we noticed an abandoned factory. I parked the Humvee on the side of the factory to avoid being seen. I told the team that I would be going radio silent from here onward.

We all split up to get into our positions. I flew out past the warehouse till I was sitting over the ocean. This was the first time I saw the ocean or a port. However, I did not have the luxury to sit around and admire it...

I had work to do, and I began to raise my mana and entered my empowered state. I stirred the winds and manipulated water in the area, creating a storm. I started to electrify the clouds I created.

Finally, once I felt it was complete, I started to head to the courtyard. I thought enough time had passed. Dylan

and the others should have them all trapped already. I just hoped that they would get out before I got there. I moved the storm directly above the courtyard.

I looked down from inside the eye of the storm and saw the smugglers trapped in the middle of the yard and my storm. Some were stunned by simply seeing my empowered state and decided to flee. A group splintered off, trying to escape. I could hear their leader, Quinn, yelling at them to stop. I let the clouds rain down on them. I began to quickly cool the temperature. Quinn's men desperately looked for an exit.

I saw that they were trying to climb out of the barriers my team had set up. I froze the rain with Ice Magic, creating thousands of tiny icicles. Quinn Hails and the rest of her group watched in horror as I ripped apart the men trying to escape with a shower of icicles. Some of the men with her group panicked and tried to make a break for it. I struck them down one by one with lightning bolts. The survivors huddled around their leader, shivering in fear.

I could see that Quinn was the only one to stand up. Her mouth was moving. It seemed like she was trying to talk to me. I lowered the earth beneath them, so they got stuck in a muddy pit. I flew down to the pit's edge to give them their only hope of survival. "If you surrender now, I will spare your lives. What's your answer!?"

In truth, the only answer I would accept was complete surrender. I saw Quinn stand up yet again; she was freezing cold, with tears running down her face.

She looked up at me in terror, the clouds rumbling behind me. Angrily, she shouted, "I was supposed to have imm—"

I cut her off by making the thunder boom overhead. It was so loud you could feel the vibrations from the thunderclaps. She had continued to plead with me.

I stood there coldly staring at her until she realized I couldn't hear her. I calmed the storm and the thunder so that Quinn could hear me speak. "My mission was to eliminate your entire gang. I am sparing your lives, so sit down and shut your mouth."

She was about to speak up again but held back. She sat down with what was left of her gang. I partially sealed the pit and began to walk away. I dispersed the storm and started to power down slowly.

I saw Dylan in the distance running towards me. Dylan glanced at the bodies of the HSR members as he made his way to me. When he got close enough, he asked me if I had killed them all. I pointed to the pit and said, "They surrendered. The bodies you saw were the ones that tried to escape."

Dylan walked over the edge of the hole and looked inside. "Woah, they look terrified. Ben, you're scary when you get serious, man."

Dylan walked back to me and gave me a radio. I contacted the rest of the team, "Congratulations, our first mission was a success. Lauren contacted the INM and told them to pick up Quinn Hails and the rest of her gang. Dylan, still awe-struck, said, "Ben, that fiery form you were in has got to be the coolest thing I've ever seen."

I smiled and said, "I'm glad you knew what the signal was."

Dylan chuckled. "right after I had disarmed them, we saw this storm just appear over the ocean. The whole team realized what the signal was."

Dylan and I met up with the rest of the team and returned to base. Gerard greeted us when we arrived. Gerard saw an INM van pull up with prisoners and cocked his head to the side.

I pulled Gerard aside and told him, "I joined the INM so that I could help people. I will not kill enemies that surrender. They should atone for their mistakes. This system was made to hold people accountable for their actions. We want them to become better people, right?"

He heard me out patiently before saying, "This system was made so we can uphold justice."

I couldn't help but agree; however, I didn't like elimination missions. "Gerard, don't assign me T4 missions anymore, please..." Gerard considered my proposal.

He laughed and told me that I was a good kid. "I'll see what I can do."

Then, another question popped into my head. "Hey Gerard, do you keep tabs on some of the people we bring in?" He raised an eyebrow.

"Not normally, no." He seemed caught off guard by the question. He wondered why I asked that, so I told him.

"I was curious to see if Jarvon was doing any better." Gerard let out a small laugh. "It's funny that you ask. Jarvon is doing better. He hasn't been using his powers to hurt anyone anymore."

I told Gerard that although Jarvon Criegs had hurt many people and was a jerk, he never actually killed anyone. "You see, people can change."

He smiled and asked if I could stop by his office tomorrow at ten A.M. I nodded and walked back to my team. We all had used a good amount of mana that night. We went to the mess hall to grab some food before bed.

I awoke the following day to Dylan knocking at my door. I wondered why he was there. Dylan told me it was quarter past ten and that Gerard sent him to wake me up.

"Oh shit, I totally forgot. Thanks, Dylan. I'll get going." Dylan headed over to the training grounds with the rest of the team. I got to

Gerard's office around 10:40.

When I walked into Gerard's office, It seemed like he was on an important call. Gerard told whomever he was talking to that I had arrived and hung up.

"Slept okay, Ben?" I smiled at him, "Like a baby."

He smiled. "While you were asleep, I had the opportunity to talk with the rest of your squad individually." I got excited and asked, "Oh, that's great. What did you talk to them about?"

Gerard tapped his fingers on his desk. "We talked about you, Ben. They all said great things about you. They told me about their time on Covenhiem."

He looked at me and grinned. "They told me what training with you was like. We also spoke about last night's mission. Dylan told me you created a storm and took on the entire HSR gang yourself."

I told Gerard that he was giving me too much credit.

"Well, Dylan had already disarmed them. The HSR had no choice but to surrender."

Gerard sat back in his chair and became a little more serious. "I spoke with the survivors of the HSR after you captured them. Only one of the survivors was brave enough to speak. I guessed, "Quinn Hails." Gerard nodded and continued.

Quinn told me that you created a category two storm and killed over twenty of her men."

I shook my head as I thought back to that night. They should have stayed where they were and surrendered. Gerard explained that he had seen footage of me when I attacked. Apparently, some security clips caught me on camera. "Ben, I didn't know you could do that. I was surprised when I saw you in that empowered state while in that practice match against your squad. Your progress is incredible. We are going to have to reevaluate your power level. That can wait. However, I wanted to call you into my office to tell you that you are a good man, and I'm proud of you."

I don't know what this feeling was, but I was happy. Is this what it's like to have a father?

"Oh, I almost forgot, Ben. I will respect your wishes. Your team will not be assigned T4 missions."

It felt like a weight had been lifted when I heard that.

"I didn't join the INM to kill people. Thank you, sir."

I left his office in a good mood. I met back with my squad at the training grounds and continued to train with them.

The following day, I had an INM agent drop an envelope in my room. It was a new mission, T3 B ranked. I called the squad to the briefing room to talk more about the mission.

Once everyone was present, I handed the file to Dylan and let him explain the mission details. He announced that the new mission was T3 B ranked and that our target was a thief who could turn invisible.

He had already stolen from museums, pawn shops, and other small businesses. Dylan came up with the idea that we should go into different areas and then radio in when we find out what location he's at. Dylan pointed out possible places he might try to steal from. So, we did just that. We split up and waited for one of us to radio in when we thought he was at our location.

After hours of waiting, Dylan was the one to radio in. Dyan sealed the exits in the building and waited. Dylan still couldn't figure out where the invisible person was. Jax was the first one to arrive. Jax started by lowering the temperature inside the shop Dylan was in.

Once the temperature dropped to freezing, Jax wandered inside to look for him. Since Jax wasn't affected by the cold, he could apprehend him without being slowed down.

Finally, Jax saw puffs of warm air exhaling from a room's corner. Jax walked up and grabbed the man without resistance.

The guy was captured before anyone else from our squad even showed up. The man's name was Andrew Hunter. We brought him back to base and told Gerard about the mission. Gerard was again impressed. It only took two of my squad members to complete the task.

We continued to train when another mission would be sent to my room every other week. Soon, all of our missions began to blur together. Our squad grew stronger and closer. This was the most fun I have had in my life. It all had to end sometime...

One day, I got a T3 S-ranked mission. Our mission was to capture a clairvoyant named Katherine Maya. The ranking was high on this mission due to the fact she was a clairvoyant. It gave her the power to get out of seemingly impossible situations. Our data told us that she could see multiple futures and pick the best outcome for herself. We received a tip on where she might be hiding. The intel was correct. When we found her, she wasn't surprised. In fact, she immediately started to run toward an industrial warehouse. Which, at the time, made me happy. Fewer civilians meant I could use a more extensive range of my powers freely. Jax chased the clairvoyant into an abandoned warehouse. Dylan and Lauren started to seal off the exits on the back side.

Sara and I stayed out front and waited to see if Maya would come running back this way. Jax radioed in,

"Hey, Captain, I can't find her. This place is enormous. I don't know, captain, something feels off."

Suddenly, Sara and I could hear these loud crashes from inside the building.

Jax came running out of the building, yelling, "Run!" I had never seen Jax run so fast in my life.

He dived behind a shipping container to take cover. I radioed Jax to find out what was going on. A giant mech suit came crashing out of the warehouse. I could see a man inside. It was Kash Johnson, the most wanted man in the INM database. The mech suit turned and started to scan the area. The mech lifted its left arm, and its right hand started to press some buttons on a control console.

Twelve large drones came flying out of the warehouse. Jax radioed that he could see that the drones were equipped with lasers and a missile.

I radioed Dylan and Lauren and told them to take care of the drones while Jax, Sara, and I fought Kash. Suddenly, the missiles on Johnson's shoulders activated, and he began launching missiles at Jax and Sara's location. Sara and I created an earth wall strong enough to absorb the blasts. Jax was able to take this opportunity to run behind Kash. I could hear loud explosions near the rooftop of the warehouse where Dylan and Lauren were. I flew up to get a better view of what was happening on the roof.

I saw Dylan covered in blood. He cried in agony and used his Metal Magic to destroy the rest of the drones. Dylan passed out from using too much mana.

I turned back to Kash and shot flames at his cockpit. I was blocking his vision as well as blocking his sensors. The mech suite had these guns that shot energy beams from its hands. I dodged the energy beams and flew over to Sara's position.

Sara and I began to shift the earth underneath its feet. The mech suite toppled over. Jax jumped on top of it and began to freeze it in place.

The circuits on the control panel started to lose power. Then the cockpit ejected, and Kash jumped out. He was holding an energy weapon like the one on the mech suit. Kash started to fire energy beams at us. I dived and dodged the deadly rays.

Kash revealed that he was also carrying graphite explosives. He threw one at me, forcing me to fly out of the blast range. The shockwave still hit me from a distance, sending me back to the floor.

He continued to throw more explosives at Sara and Jax. They were pinned down behind an earth shield Sara created. I needed to be more cautious about those bombs.

They are more potent than I expected. Jax was throwing ice spears at Kash, but to no avail. Jax began to freeze the floor and create ice walls to block the exits. Kash ran towards an ice wall and threw an explosive, making a hole for him to slide underneath and keep moving.

Sara was out of range and did not have a gap closer. I flew over to Kash's location and blocked his path. Alex's hand patted my arm and asked, "Did you kill him?" I looked over at Alex.

"No, I needed him alive so that he could fix the INM satellites... He ended up killing himself." I continued with the memories of that night. Kash started to reach for his ray gun when I used Metal Magic and pulled the weapon out of his hands, or so I thought. I took a step forward when Kash reached out an arm and told me to stay right there.

Unexpectedly, Kash yelled out, "You have already lost! You just haven't realized it yet! The INM cannot win. It doesn't matter if I live or die here!" Kash grinned, "this is a plastic explosive." I clenched my teeth. I should have known the bastard was hiding something.

We were at a stalemate for the moment, but I had the advantage. I still had Jax and Sara on their way. Kash smiled at me and spoke again. "I've seen the footage before deleting it. I know the truth! The clairvoyant told me I would return in the future." He armed the explosive in his hand. I shook my head in disbelief, "He wouldn't."

At that moment I thought, He's going to do it... I could tell this bomb was even bigger than the others. I have to get out of here!

I flew up into the air and watched him detonate it. I had to fly higher and higher to escape the blast radius. I saw his death with my own eyes.

I went back and collected the rest of my team.

I was met with even worse news: Sara was sitting down crying. Jax walked over carrying Dylan, who was still unconscious. I looked around for Lauren when Jax told me she was gone. I asked where she was, and Jax told me, "A few places." It finally hit me: the blood that was on Dylan wasn't his own.

Lauren must have died when they were attacking the drones. I yelled out into the sky in frustration. Memories of my first mission came flooding back. I focused on my breathing and tried to stay calm. Sara walked over and held me.

She said, "Ben, I know you are in pain, but there is still someone who needs you right now."

Sara pointed to Dylan, and my heart sank. This whole mission was a disaster... We got in the Humvee and headed back to base. The first thing we did was head to the infirmary.

We left Dylan in the infirmary overnight. Jax pulled up a chair and stayed with Dylan. Sara and I headed back to my room. We were both tired and depressed.

Sara and Lauren had just started to become close. Dylan and Lauren were more than just friends. I began to think about what would have happened if I had lost Sara.

I couldn't imagine the pain Dylan is enduring right now. He must have witnessed it firsthand. Sara held me tightly. I could feel her trembling.

I felt nothing now, just this lingering numbness. I don't know when I fell asleep. I just know that I had no dreams that night.

When I woke, I didn't feel rested. I felt just as tired as I did before I had fallen asleep. Gerard came by my room and asked me to tell him about the mission and what happened. I told him everything. Gerard took notes and apologized for our loss.

"This has been an unfortunate turn of events. We really needed Kash alive to fix our satellites. Get some rest, Ben. You and your team need time to mourn."

A few hours later, I got a call from Jax that Dylan had woken up. Jax told me that Dylan wasn't talking to anyone or eating his food. I told Jax to give him time and space.

We held a funeral for Lauren. Dylan was there, but he looked the same way I looked after I failed my first mission.

After the funeral, Gerard contacted me to ask about Dylan. He noticed that Dylan seemed more distant and depressed than the others. I told him that the two were very close. They loved each other.

Gerard nodded. "This is why dating people within your same division or squad isn't allowed."

I couldn't help but agree.

"Yeah, I see that now, "Gerard mentioned that my team and I had to go through another evaluation test. He told me he would give us a week to prepare ourselves.

I went back to my team to tell them the news about the evaluation tests. At the time, no one really seemed to care. We were all still feeling pretty down. Jax came up to me in private.

"Captain, out of forty-two missions, only two of them have been considered failures. That is a twenty-one to one ratio, thats the highest ratio in the INM. These things were bound to happen sooner or later. I think you're a great Captain, for what it's worth."

I thanked Jax. I really needed to hear that. Alex stopped me to ask a question.

"I noticed that Quinn Hails and Kash Johnson were trying to tell you something. I countered and explained that both were criminals. Quinn ran a human smuggling ring, and Kash hacked military satellites.

The last thing I should do is listen to them." Alex scratched his head.

"I guess you're right," I explained, that the Necromancer I had to deal with was crazy. Of all the assignments I've been on, the people I was ordered to capture were either insane or had abused their powers.

If I started listening to them, it would just get in the way of completing my missions. Alex nodded, "that makes sense, I guess."

I started to share the memories of what happened next. I made my way to Dylan's room to check on him. I knocked on the door, and a moment later, Dylan answered.

"Captain? What are you doing here?" I told him I wanted to see how he was doing. "May I come in?" Dylan nodded and closed the door behind me. Dylan asked if I wanted anything to drink. I smiled and pulled out a bottle of whiskey from inside my jacket.

Dylan cocked his head to the side and asked, "Where did you find that?" I laughed. "I saw it in Gerard's office beside some other drinks." Dylan had a worried and shocked expression.

"Captain, you're something else." Dylan laughed and got out a couple of glasses. I poured us a drink, and we knocked it back. It was smooth and made your body warm up quickly.

"Dylan, I know that you and Lauren were really close... I am sorry, truly." Dylan was silent for a moment.

"Lauren and I were fighting the drones on the rooftops. The drones were all spread out, and we had difficulty shooting them down. We were dodging the lasers, but suddenly, all the drones shot their missiles at the same time. I could force the missiles coming at me in a different direction.

But when I turned to see if Lauren was okay, I saw several missiles land right next to her. I saw her die in front of me. I wasn't powerful enough to save her. After she died, the drones started to get closer to me, just close enough to where I could use Metal Magic on all of them."

Dylan was clenching his fists and crying. I poured us another drink. "Dylan, you're a good man and an even better friend. We'll get through this together."

I raised my glass, and we toasted and finished another drink.

"Captain, I don't blame you for what happened. In fact, I don't know what I'd do without you. You are like the older brother I've always wanted."

I gave Dylan a hug and told him to get some rest. I headed to Sara's room. There was something I wanted to talk to her about.

I knocked on her door, and she greeted me with a kiss. I walked over and sat her down at a small table in the room.

Her smile faded. She knew something was off by my body language. I told her that I wanted to put our relationship on hold. I've seen Dylan's pain, and I didn't wish that for either of us.

"Look, Sara, I care about you. I don't want you to suffer like that." I knew she didn't like the idea of splitting up.

"Ben, I care about you too... I understand how you feel, and I know you're trying to protect me. I'll be here when you're ready." I gave her one last kiss before pulling myself away from her. "Good night, Sara."

I returned to my room. My day had felt so long. I heard a chime and looked at my phone. Gerard messaged me that Jax and Sara's evaluation tests would be this Wednesday. Dylan and I will have our test this Thursday.

I continued to train and expand my powers. I pushed myself every time I thought back on my regrets. I exhausted myself a lot that day. Finally, Wednesday came.

I decided to conserve as much energy as I could. I slept in, ate a large meal, and went for a brief jog. I napped during the afternoon to get as much rest as I could.

Later that night, Jax and Sara returned exhausted. I could tell they really gave it their all. Both of them went straight to their rooms and passed out. I was sure that Sara was still upset with me over our talk, so I gave her some space.

Gerard sent me another message saying Dylan and I would have our evaluation at a different facility. The following day, Dylan and I had a transport take us to our test site.

We were in the transport vehicle for hours until we pulled up to a large, almost abandoned-looking building. There were very few guards and INM agents. We were escorted to a waiting room until Gerard arrived and took Dylan to the evaluation site. I was dying of boredom. I had been waiting for two hours.

Dylan came out just as tired as the others. Gerard came to take me to the evaluation site. Gerard seemed annoyed, though. He was muttering, "What the hell... why did she choose this location?"

I asked who Gerard was referring to, and he told me there was a high-level administrator in the INM who was interested in seeing my full power.

Gerard said, "This test is essential. The admin's name is Rebecca. She's already waiting for us."

Chapter 8: Promotion

Gerard and I walked into a large room with a huge glass window. I looked out the window and saw the test site. It was a large stadium. It seemed to be an old Human Spirit building. A popular gaming center for physical sports and events. It looked empty, with a mixture of dirt and grass. It also looked like there were some people inside. There were no real trees or vegetation that I could see.

Gerard said, "Hey, you'll get a better look later...let's go." Finally, we reached the end of a hall leading to a room.

This beautiful woman was sitting in a chair with her tablet. She looked up, a little confused, and turned to Gerard.

She didn't say anything, though. She leaned back in her chair and stared at me. It felt like she was studying me, the way her eyes moved around.

She put her hand on her chin and looked at Gerard. It was weird how quiet it was; thankfully, Gerard broke the silence and announced. "Ben, this is Rebecca."

I stepped forward to shake her hand, but she just sat there.

"Sorry," she exclaimed. "I don't shake hands." She stood up and smiled; she was about five foot seven inches.

"I've heard a lot about you, Ben. Gerard speaks highly of you." Gerard nodded at me and said, "He's got talent." It felt good to know Gerard had my back. Rebecca pulled up my INM file on her tablet. She gestured to me to stand next to her and take a look. "Okay, I will be showing you your first evaluation exam when you first joined the INM. She began to read off my results. I had never seen the scores, so I needed to figure out what to make of them.

B in single-target attacks

C in close combat

C in ranged combat

D in AOE abilities (Area of Effect)

C in endurance

C in defense

C in speed

B in mana capacity

Your overall score was a B ranking." She continued to read off a list of my abilities, "You know, lightning, earth, fire, water, and wind. Your first mission ended in disaster. Not only did you fail, but five of your teammates died. However, Gerard saw your potential. We overlooked this because you could have completed the mission independently, so we decided to give you a chance to advance. Since you've been Captain, you have been on 42 missions with two fails. That's a good record." She raised an eyebrow and looked at the details as to why I failed the two missions. "Also, the stats of everyone on your team have improved dramatically. This is impressive, considering an average captain would lose one to two squad members after about ten missions. You see, Ben, many of our fellow INM members have not improved. We would like to see what your stats look like compared to your first evaluation." Gerard looked over at me.

"It's time."

Gerard walked me to the evaluation area to begin my test. I noticed the bodies I saw inside were multiple ballistic gel dummies set up in different places. Gerard reminded me, "Ben, you've seen how we grade people's tests. give it your all and show us what you can do." Deep down, I wanted to make Gerard proud.

Honestly, not even I know what I'm capable of. I walked out into the middle of the field and waited for the signal.

I heard a loud buzzer go off and instantly began intensifying my mana. First, I increased my body temperature and went into my empowered form. I jumped up and blasted myself into the air. I started by generating gale-force winds; the facility walls barely contained my power. I created a large tornado, destroying all of the gel dummies in moments. I could have made a stronger tornado, but I had to keep my power under control. I didn't want to risk destroying the facility and hurting everyone inside. I took a deep breath and let out a fierce fire stream from inside the heart of the tornado. I created a firestorm incinerating everything within the testing area; even the walls were blackened and singed. I slowed down the winds to show more of my other abilities. I used a large amount of mana and raised a forty-foot earth wall. I started to gather a large amount of electrical energy. I channeled all the electricity to the palms of my hands.

I condensed the energy into a single form... A lightning javelin with extraordinary power. I pulled my arm back and launched my javelin weapon at the earth wall I had created. The javelin spear moved at the speed of lightning, making it nearly unavoidable. It pierced straight through the wall. A moment later, we heard an explosion. I powered down and ran outside to make sure no one was hurt.

Gerard and Rebecca walked over to inspect the damage I had done. My javelin had gone through my earth wall and the facility's walls and hit a shipping container.

Rebecca and Gerard could barely find remnants of the ballistic dummies. Rebecca looked at me and asked me to make an earth chair and table. I had just enough energy to fulfill her request. She pulled out her tablet and sat there momentarily, inputting some calculations. Rebecca glanced at Gerard and nodded; she handed Gerard the tablet so he could see the new scores. Gerard studied my results carefully and said, "This is a fair assessment."

Gerard then handed me my new test scores so that I could see them.

S in single-target attacks

A in close combat

A in ranged combat

S in AOE abilities

A in endurance

A in defense

A in speed

S in mana capacity

Gerard notified Rebecca that she did not see my full capabilities. Gerard updated my file, showing the complete list of my abilities. It read lightning, earth, fire, water, wind, metal, ice, and Enhanced Lightning manipulation. Rebecca looked at Gerard and then at me.

"Huh, a walking natural disaster. You destroyed all fifty ballistic dummies in under a minute using just the regular tornado, then completely incinerated them with that firestorm.

Your lightning attack was not only powerful but fast. Rebecca turned her head to Gerard and said, "Gerard, would you like to be the one to tell him?" Gerard looked at me with a big smile. "Congratulations, Ben, you're being promoted."

I was stunned; I didn't know what to think. I asked, "Promoted to what?" Gerard smiled. "My position, Major General."

I first thought about my team. "What will happen to my squad?" Rebecca spoke up. "Both Dylan and Jax scored high enough to become captains themselves. Curious, I asked, "What about Sara?" Rebecca explained that she didn't score as high but still had some options open to her."

I asked what my new duties would be if I accepted this promotion. Gerard told me that I would have two things that they needed me to do.

The first would be to train recruits since I did well with my team. The second would be defending the base where I'm stationed.

Rebecca could tell I was conflicted. She could see that I didn't want to leave my team. "Ben, you're looking at this all wrong. Your whole team is getting promoted; this is a good thing. The INM needs strong people like you." Then Gerard cut into the conversation, "There is an INM base that needs your help. It's located in a coastal region. It gets terrible storms, and there are two cities that dislike our presence there. We cannot afford to lose that base; we need you to hold down the fort and maintain the peace in the region."

Deep down, I just wanted to stay the Captain of my team. I know that I told Sara I wanted to put our relationship on hold, but now I won't be able to see her at all...

Rebecca told me that Dylan and Jax had already accepted their new positions as captains. They would be under Rebecca's direct command.

Rebecca told me that as Major General, I would also get a personal secretary at the INM base I would command. Rebecca also informed me that, although Sara did not qualify to be a captain, she could accept the role of secretary. It felt like a weight had been lifted off my chest.

At least I won't be alone. Gerard said, "Ben, we can talk about the details later. I'm happy for ya."

I thanked them for the promotion and headed back to the car. Dylan and I both fell asleep the whole way back. Once we got back, we headed to our rooms. It was late, and I was still tired.

It was a quiet night; I wasn't feeling like myself. I was zoning out when I heard a knock on the door. When I opened the door, Sara stood there with a worried expression. "Ben, I heard we aren't on the same team anymore."

"Is that true?" I looked into her beautiful green eyes; she was scared and confused. I told her that, "Dylan and Jax got promoted, too. They will form squads of their own and go on their own missions." Sara was frustrated and said, "Jax told me the same thing; he also told me that you got a big promotion as well.

Ben, I'm going to be left behind!" Sara was on the brink of tears. I tried my best to comfort her.

"Sara, we should be happy for them; they got promoted because we all got strong together. Sara, don't worry; it's not like we'll ever see them again. One day, we will all get together and laugh about the good times when we were a team. I also heard that you did well on your evaluation. Even if the test admin doesn't see it, you're just as strong as Jax and Dylan."

I started to think back to what Rebecca had told me. Sara could be my secretary at the new base. She would also be out of danger, and we could be together again.

"Speaking of the test admin, she also told me something else."

Sara was curious and asked, "What do you mean?"

"I was told that you qualify to become my aid, my secretary at the base. "Sara's eyes began to tear up. "You want me to come with you?" I got closer to her and held her in my arms.

"You know I do." I leaned in and kissed her, and she kissed me back. I never realized I could love someone so much; we slept together that night.

I woke up early the following day to start my morning exercises. Gerard came by the training grounds to tell me that Dylan and Jax had already gone to different INM bases to create their Squads. It felt like everything was happening so fast.

I told Gerard that Sara would be accepting the secretary position under me.

"That's good, Ben. I know you like her." I got embarrassed for a moment.

"Come on, Gerard, do you have to say it."

Gerard laughed momentarily, then said, "Ben, I know this might feel like it's happening too fast. I wish I could defend that base, but I don't have the same abilities you do. I have other duties; I am now second in command of the INM."

I was grateful to Gerard. He was like the father I never had. Gerard told me he was going to head back to his office so that he could get Sara appointed as my secretary.

He told me to pack our bags; we would leave tomorrow night. When I got to my room, I looked at my phone.

I was still worried about Dylan; I didn't get time to help him mend his wounds. I knew he was still hurting; I called him to see how he was doing.

The phone rang, and he answered, "Hey, Captain, congrats on becoming a Major." I laughed. "I was just calling to congratulate you." Dylan was happy to hear from me; he still seemed depressed.

"It's good to hear your voice, sir. I was just in the middle of looking for candidates to be on my squad. Why did you pick us?" I explained, "All of you had powers that I did not; I had thought maybe I could learn from you guys, and maybe you could learn something from me." Dylan gave it some thought.

"That's pretty good advice. I mean, it worked out after all. Oh, I meant to ask, what will happen to Sara?" I told him Sara would be my secretary at my new location.

I didn't realize what I said would hurt him. Dylan spoke softly. "That's good, Ben. She really loves you. I'm happy for ya. Hey, uh, I got to make my selections; thanks for the advice." we said our goodbyes and hung up. I went back to packing my bags and getting ready for tomorrow. I woke up early and did my normal routine.

Sara and I met for breakfast. She told me she was still nervous about going to a different region of the world. She never really traveled, and she was timid. Now, she had to move somewhere she had no knowledge of, and the only person she would know was me.

I told her everything would be okay; we had to adapt when we lived in Covenhiem. This would be no different. We got a car to take us to a private INM airbase. I had never been on a plane before. So, I found the whole experience fascinating. We got on our plane and flew for hours. I haven't ravelled as much as I would have wanted, so being able to see the world's oceans and different regions during the flight was excellent. Sara passed the time reading a book on medicinal herbs. I ended up passing out halfway through the flight. Sara woke me up and told me that we had arrived. She pointed out a large forest and, in the distance, the INM base that would soon be mine.

Chapter 9: The Wolves

I was more interested in the forest than the base at the time. Sara was also excited to see what vegetation and herbs she could find. The pilot warned that the weather near the base would be bumpy.

We endured some turbulence but ended up landing okay. Sara and I exited the plane and started to head to the INM base. An INM agent was sent to welcome us.

"Welcome, General Cardovic. My name is Mason Bass. This is INM base twenty-seven we..."

I stopped him right there and apologized. "My apologies; there is a storm heading this way. Sara, get a tour of this facility in the meantime," I entered my empowered form and flew towards the storm.

There was that time when I went over the ocean during my mission to eliminate Quinn, but I didn't get the time to appreciate it.

I flew straight into the eye of the storm; I could feel the cold rain patter against my heated body. The strong winds are pulling at me.

This was the biggest, most significant natural storm I've encountered. I basked in its power and let my mana flow through it. It was incredible; I could feel everything within it. I began to use my power to hold the storm back from crashing into the base. I thought to myself, "This is why I was sent here." I slowed the winds and dispersed the clouds. I calmed the sea and hovered there in silence. I bathed in the serenity of that moment, knowing that the storm's power was now mine.

I had used a lot of mana and began to feel weary. I returned to the INM base and was greeted by Sara at the front entrance. Sara handed me new clothes as I landed since I would constantly weather them.

Sara smiled, "These clothes were a gift from Gerard. He told me that he had some INM scientists create weather-resistant clothing for you." I was impressed it looked durable.

Sara watched me as I put my new clothes on. She said, "It looks good on you. To be honest, I thought you were going to be out there all day." Sara looked at her phone. "You were out there for two whole hours; you look tired." She could sense that I was low on mana.

Sara had already finished her base tour; she decided it was best to get me some food. We made our way to the mess hall; we couldn't help but notice everyone was staring at us. After we ate, Sara showed me to my room. I didn't realize how much energy I had used to eliminate that storm. I flopped face-first onto my new bed. Sara sat beside me and said, "You look down, Ben." I rolled over till I was lying on my back. I looked over at Sara and stared into her eyes. "I don't know what I'd do without you."

Sara mentioned that she had never seen me like this. Confused, I asked, "Like what?" She quietly said, "Vulnerable." Sara reached for her satchel and looked around for a moment. She pulled out some odd-looking plant that I had never seen before.

She said, "This is a rare type of Rhodiola plant; it was recently discovered that it could restore mana. Some INM scientists sent me a sample, so I started to grow and study them." Sara put the plant's root on the upper right side of my chest. Her green eyes began to glimmer and shine; she had started to use her Plant Magic on the Rhodiola. It was a strange sensation; I could feel the roots latching onto me. I could feel this warmth coming from the plant; Sara had one hand on the Rhodiola and the other hand on my chest. The Rhodiola flower was white but started to change colors. The flower began to glow and turn a bright purple.

Then it hit me; my mana was being restored rapidly. Some of my fatigue had started to fade away in moments. Sara plucked a couple of the petals, she put one in her mouth and ate it. She reached over and put the other purple Rhodiola petal into my mouth. The petal just tasted like a normal regular flower petal. Confused, I asked, "If the Rhodiola root can restore mana and physical stamina, what do the petals do? Sara smiled at me and said, "It's an aphrodisiac."

She leaned in and kissed me. I'm not sure what came over me, but she seemed more beautiful than usual.

She stared into my eyes when I asked, "What's an aphrodisiac?" Sara let out a cute laugh and kissed me again.

The rest of the night was a blur. It was so strange because I woke up more tired than when I had dispersed the storm. But I had a job to do. I started to check out the base when I ran into Mason Bass again.

He finally got the chance to introduce himself properly. After shaking hands and talking to him for a few minutes, Sara joined us in the hall. Sara told Mr. Bass she would give me a real base tour. Sara and I used our Earth Magic to sense the structural layout of the facility. Sara told me that as my secretary, it is her duty to inform me on of the current state of the base. She explained that I should give an announcement to the INM agents stationed here. Sara sent out a memo for the INM Agents to gather at the training area in three hours.

We arrived thirty minutes early to prepare; Sara placed a small mic on my shirt and created a raised earth platform. A few hundred INM agents were either there or at least listening in if they could not be there physically.

I introduced myself. "Hello, my name is Benjamin Cardovic. I was sent here to calm the seas as well as our enemies. I am here to uphold justice and ensure peace. I have experienced loss and failure, and I no longer fear either. From this day onward, we will train and live together as brothers on this base. I am the Major General of this INM base, and starting tomorrow, all Captains, bring your squads here at 0500."

I began to leave the podium when I spotted a familiar face.

"Dante?" I walked over to him to see what he was doing there. He stared at me almost as if he was worried.

I asked if he was okay, and his response wasn't what I expected. "You seem so different compared to the last time we met. Ever since I met you, I've been seeing a black wolf in my dreams. Your eyes haven't changed, those piercing amber eyes. I don't know what you have done to yourself, but I can tell my magic won't transform you into anything. Dante was studying me. "Have you become more human?" Dante spoke in metaphors, and it sounded kind of cryptic.

However, I understood what he was saying. Sara stood back and watched with some level of concern. I asked Dante to raise his mana as high as he could so that I could gauge his mana capacity. It seemed he was around a high B to a low A. It was noticeable he had gotten stronger.

However, he should be stronger than this.

Dante said, "I am a Captain under your command, General. If you don't mind me asking I have a question for you." I nodded, curious to see what he would ask.

"How did you become so strong? What did you do? I have been training like mad but don't feel like I have been improving recently." I chuckled momentarily and repeated, "Training starts at 0500 hours; I'll show you."

Dante's face lit up with excitement; Dante grinned and walked off. Sara asked who Dante was, so I gave her the short version. I explained that I met him when I first joined the INM. We weren't friends or anything, but we had a mutual respect for one another. Sara and I got back to the office.

"I am sending out a memo telling all INM squads to halt training for today and conserve mana tomorrow.

Curiously, Sara asked, "What kind of training do you have planned for tomorrow?"

I told Sara that I would train them in a similar manner to how I trained her. I would display my powers and instruct them. With time and practice, they could learn something.

Sara smiled, remembering fond memories of us training together. I kissed her goodnight and told her to get some sleep; I just wanted to go to bed early. If she didn't go to her room, I'd never get rest. I woke up the following day overflowing with mana.

When I arrived at the training grounds, I saw Dante already getting the rest of the men in order. I wanted the men focused and heated like a well-oiled machine. I told them to follow me; I already knew where I wanted to train the men. There was a forest on the other side of the base I still wanted to check out. I had the men follow me for a few miles until we reached a clearing in the woods. The forest was very different from Covenhiem; I found it all fascinating. I took a look around while I let the men rest.

It was warm out with some cloud coverage; I had the men line up facing me. "For those who do not know who I am, I am the greatest elemental mage in the INM. I will be demonstrating my Elemental Magic to all of you. I do not expect you to learn all my abilities; however, this is an opportunity to learn some aspect of my powers, if not more. Build up your mana, and take a deep breath until the air reaches your diaphragms. Move that energy up to your chest, and use the heat from your body to heat your breath.

As you start to exhale, ignite the air in your breath. I showed them and shot a large stream of fire into the air. The men studied me with their jaws open in amazement.

I watched as they all attempted to breathe fire. They nearly all failed on their first attempt. Dante, however, shot out a small stream of fire.

Dante's eyes lit up with excitement. Dante roared, took another deep breath, and shot out a larger flame breath. One by one, I demonstrated my different abilities.

Most failed, but a couple started to pick up an Elemental Magic. Dante became frustrated because the only power he could learn was flame breath. We trained for hours until we were exhausted. I told them that our training for the day was over and that we would pick it up tomorrow. I started to jog back to base; I could hear the men groaning behind me, trying to keep up. This continued for days until I noticed something off with Dante. I had just finished demonstrating Lightning Magic when I saw Dante getting rattled. Dante was having trouble shooting lightning bolts. He could electrically charge his body in a way I hadn't seen before. I called out to Dante to keep that electrical current going. I could see that his body was still charged; he may not be able to shoot lightning bolts, but maybe he's capable of something else. I yelled out, "Dante, Run!" Dante's body moved incredibly fast. He was a big guy, sitting at six feet four inches.

Dante could charge his body with electrical energy to enhance his speed and process information faster. Which in turn gave him a better reaction speed. Honestly, I was impressed. I had never seen or thought this was possible.

I stood beside him and charged my body as well. I looked at Dante, and said, "Now, let's do this together." Dante and I sprinted to the base and made it there in half the time. Winded, we took a moment to catch our breath. Dante thanked me and told me he meant to talk to me privately. Dante revealed that his visions had started to intensify since we first met. He told me, "I keep seeing a huge black wolf staring at me... with every pant, it released flames, and its shiny black coat sparked with electricity."

I asked, "When did you say these visions started?" Dante said, "I've always had visions, but none like this."

The first vision of a wolf was when he saw me at my aptitude test.

Dante finally explained why he didn't go through with the fight that day when I joined the INM. "I stood in the stands, ready to watch your aptitude exam. Usually, I'm pretty good at guessing what my power could transform someone into. I had a hard time trying to pinpoint yours, though. It was an animal I hadn't seen anyone else transform into yet. You were fearless and hungry for battle. Your eyes were cold, and your amber glare focused on me. You smiled at me like you were excited to fight. I witnessed your raw talent for myself that day; then it hit me."

Visions of a white wolf in the darkness and the sound of a low rumbling echoed. I couldn't tell if it was the sound of thunder or a low growling. Even if I had transformed you during our fight, all that would do is transform you into a wolf. Not only that, but you could still use your elemental powers in that wolf-like state. I would have made you stronger and even more vicious. There was no victory for me. After I backed down from our fight, I started to see visions and have recurring dreams.

When I looked in the mirror, sometimes I could see that large black wolf staring back at me. "Dante, I have some thoughts about what you have been going through. You said that when you saw me at my aptitude test, you saw a white wolf in the dark. But when you looked in a mirror, you saw a black wolf."

I thought about it some more and then asked, "I know your original power is transforming people into other creatures, but have you ever used it on yourself?"

Dante shook his head. "What if I use it on myself and I'm unable to change back, or..." I cut him off.

"Are you afraid of your own power? This is why we are here. Test out this theory of yours and use your magic on yourself." Dante hesitated momentarily, but with a sudden grunt, his body started to transform. I watched his transformation until I saw a large black wolf, just as he described.

Dante looked around first at the world, then at his paws. he jumped around excitedly and started panting. His coat shimmered with electrical sparks; his speed was still augmented while in his wolf form.

He seemed both happy and excited. He shot out a large fire breath and burned a tree to ash. Dante started reverting to his human form. He looked at his hands.

"I should have done this long ago...Thank you, General."

I was happy for Dante; it must have been a struggle for him. I was proud that he advanced his ability further. Once I had gotten back to my room, I brought out some notes I had been taking. I noticed that nearly all of them had picked up some aspect of my power.

They were also helping each other out and working together. They were all growing stronger. I had called Sara to set up a buffet for the men; I wanted them to know I recognized their hard work.

We all got together and enjoyed our feast. Dante tilted his head, he was looking at the men in an odd way. The INM agents were all cheerful and in high spirits, but it seemed like Dante was seeing something else. I asked him what it was, and he shook his head curiously. I had the men train the next day separately. I had been getting reports that a storm would be rolling in soon.

I would casually fly out and disperse them to make things easy. I couldn't help but think, what if I wasn't here?

The base would be getting hit with constant storms. I decided to build a large earth wall, the biggest one I had ever created. It was a wall that separated the base from the sea. If a tidal wave or enemy attack got past me, another line of defense would exist. Not to mention, it was good practice for me.

I got missions from our intel division I could hand out. I assigned our Captains to fitting missions, and time began to fly by.

Sara and I were happy, and Dante became a close friend. Months went by, life became empty and boring to me. I remember being a Captain with Dylan, Jax, Lauren, and Sara.

I tried to call Dylan a few times, but he was always out on a mission

One day, I could overhear the whole base talking. Rumors were spreading around that the fabled Necromancer had resurfaced. I blocked these out and continued focusing on my powers and training my men. The Necromancer was taking refuge in Breon, where the mage named Light stayed. Light has other mages working with him to resist the INM. He is considered an S-ranked criminal; he is capable of manipulating Light as his weapon.

He had killed entire squads by himself; he could teleport at the speed of Light and shoot deadly energy rays. Light was a dangerous man and near impossible to capture.

Now, both Light and the Necromancer are working together. I told Sara to keep me updated on the situation.

One day, Sara barged into my room at two am; whatever it was, it must have been bad. Sara was already crying and carrying a handful of documents. Sara told me there was an attack on an INM base near Breon. One hundred and ten were killed, and forty were injured.

The assailants were Light and the Necromancer. This news disturbed me greatly; however, that wasn't the worst. Dylan had been killed in the attack. My heart sank, and my eyes teared up. I was in disbelief; Dylan was strong and intelligent. I had a hard time seeing him lose to anyone in battle.

I read the reports myself to find out what had happened. It mainly spoke about the Necromancer entering the INM base and attacking everyone. I was so depressed that I would unconsciously create a constant rain cloud over our base. I couldn't help but think about the young man I trained, my friend, and my brother.

This anger building inside me made the clouds roar with thunder. Weeks passed, and my sadness subsided. A lingering anger simmered just below the surface.

While helping the men with their training, I noticed them whispering. I saw Dante talking to his Lieutenant about the Necromancer. Dante looked over at me. He seemed afraid.

I asked Dante what was going on and why I was being left out of the loop. Dante clenched his teeth and shook his head.

He was trying to avoid eye contact. I had never seen him like this. I looked him in the eye and asked, "Dante, tell me what's going on."

Dante was breathing shakily. "General, we have spies in the city of Breon; it was just reported that Dylan was spotted."

At first, I was happy. I thought that maybe the report was wrong, "is it possible Dylan wasn't killed that day?"

Dante couldn't look me in the eye. "There's something more than that." Dante was breathing deeply. He kept his head down.

"The Necromancer revived Dylan."

I was confused. "What? Why? Why would he bring…"

Dante stopped me. "The Necromancer revived Dylan and killed him again."

My mind went blank. "He did what?"

I lost control of my mana. It began to flare off of me wildly, and my anger exploded.

It was the only emotion I could feel.

I looked over to at Dante and saw him mumbling something. He was looking at me wide-eyed he could see something that I could not, he was seeing a vision. I asked, "Tell me, what do you see?" Dante was panicked but began to speak clearly.

"I see it! This is what I was afraid of when I first saw you. The Great Wolf of Covenhiem! Its growl made the clouds rumble. Its amber eyes were fierce with a hunger behind them. It brings the storm. I see you now! What you would become if I tried to transform you. It terrifies me…"

I thanked Dante for telling me the truth about Dylan, even if it was harsh. I told him not to follow me and began to fly from the forest towards the sea.

Dante's words echoed in my mind, and images of Dylan's smiling face was in the forefront of my mind. I should have been there for him... Before I knew it, I was hovering over the sea close to the base.

I didn't even need to think. My emotions themselves started to create a storm; my fury manifested itself. In the corner of my eye, I spotted something. I flew over and saw eight warships heading toward my base.

I used the storm I created to entrap the warships. I needed to know who they were and what they were planning to do. I was annoyed because I wanted to let loose and pour out my rage. They were just in the way... I flew down quickly to inspect the warships. It seems like four of the ships came from the island of Alistien. The other four came from the port of Fullerken, located south of my INM base. The emblems on the ships quickly gave them away.

I flew over to the flagship and was met by regular uniformed soldiers with no magic. They all started to pull out their guns, with me as their target.

I used Metal Magic and threw their guns into the sea. The soldiers were all shocked; most had never seen magic. They were staring at me, mesmerized by my empowered state.

My body was like a furnace with electrical sparks occasionally discharging from me. My feet scorched the ship's metal floor; to them, my appearance must have looked otherworldly, perhaps even godly. An older man stepped forward and asked, "Who are you?" I am the storm... the Wolf of Covenhiem, Major General in command of the INM base these ships are headed toward. My name is Benjamin Cardovic."

A younger soldier stepped forward and yelled out, "Captain!" almost as if to ask (what do we do?)

I repeated the word slowly, "Captain?" I stared back at the older man, realizing now that he was the Captain.

I walked up and looked him in the eyes. "I used to be a Captain once... I know what it's like to be responsible for the lives of my men. I still remember the ones that I've lost. A little while ago, I discovered a close friend of mine had been killed twice now thanks to a Necromancer. I had come out here so that I could let my emotions out. This is not your typical storm surrounding your fleet. I could create hundred-foot tsunamis, maelstroms strong enough to sink every one of your ships. Storms so powerful I could destroy an armada."

His men were silent; they knew the position they were in. I made the clouds rumble and the waves increasingly violent to prove a point. The Captain gritted his teeth in frustration. There was nothing he could do... he was powerless.

The Captain looked back at the faces of his crew and then turned towards the other warships.

I stepped closer and asked, "Save them, please..."

The old Captain nodded, accepting whatever fate I chose for them. I spoke loudly, "Return to your homes and tell your people to go further inland. There is a storm coming."

I allowed the ships to return to their respective ports. As soon as they were gone, my emotions took over. I let the pain that was bottled up in my heart pour out. My screams of anguish created the biggest storm I had ever made.

It raged on until my anger turned into a melancholy numbness. When I was close to being completely out of mana, I dispersed the storm and flew back to base. As I roamed around, I noticed that the earth wall I created to shield the base was destroyed. As I landed, Sara came running out. She seemed scared. She didn't say anything, though. She held me tightly and walked me back to my room. I told her everything that happened; she had heard from Dante what had happened to Dylan and why I ran off. She knew I was in pain.

She stayed with me and saved me from my loneliness. I passed out from exhaustion. When I woke up, I went to the mess hall; the food I usually liked didn't taste like anything I could barely eat. I could hear my fellow INM agents chatter about last night. Dante sat next to me and started to eat. I looked up at Dante, who was still shaken, and asked, "Do you still see me as a wolf?"

Dante answered with a decisive "Yes."

I nodded, and we ate in silence for a little while.

Dante couldn't help but ask, "Did you create that storm last night?"

I told him I didn't want to talk about it now. Dante respected that and finished his plate. Sara walked into the mess hall in a hurry.

"Ben, I've been trying to reach you all morning."

I had left my phone in my room; I didn't feel like talking to anyone. She escorted me to my office and pulled out her tablet.

Sara looked up some news articles about the storm I had created. "Ben, the storm you created last night destroyed the port of Alistien. Luckily, the people evacuated in time, so there were no fatalities. Scientists are saying that this was one of the biggest storms in this region's history."

Sara showed me today's paper, saying that this was a horrible natural disaster. She explained that she spoke with Gerard, and he told the newspapers to call it a natural disaster. "Look, Ben, the city that's next to our base is called Standon. From what I hear, they actually like you. They call our base the Wolf's Mountain. But we don't want the public to be afraid of you. There is no mention of the warships. Guess we should have expected that."

Sara also wanted to add another piece of info.

"There is more bad news…"

Confused, I tilted my head and looked at her.

"Wait, what's the bad news?" Even though she was my secretary, Sara had received a mission from Gerard.

"I don't know the details of my mission or how long it will be. Gerard said he would fill me in when he arrives."

I asked if there was anything else that I should be aware of. Sara was saddened. "No, Ben, that's about it.

Sara asked, "What are you going to do now?"

One thing I needed to do was to repair that earth wall I accidentally destroyed, so that was the plan for now. Sara kissed me and left to report to Gerard. I spent the rest of the day recovering. Once I had the energy, I started to repair the earth wall to its former glory until Sara showed up with Gerard.

When Gerard got closer, I did notice he looked a bit younger. When he got close enough, he reached out to shake my hand. Instead, I hugged him and told him, "It's been too long, my friend." Gerard smiled, handed Sara an envelope, and told her to go prepare. Gerard and I walked to an empty room where he pulled out an expensive whiskey and two glasses. Gerard sat down and let out a sigh.

"I heard about Dylan... I know you guys were close. My deepest condolences." I nodded. "He was a good kid."

Gerard raised his glass, and we both drank at the same time.

Gerard poured another glass and said, "I need you to lay low. That storm you caused attracted a lot of attention." Gerard and I finished our second drink.

"Ben, I need you at Base thirty-two. We are worried there might be another attack," Gerard told me that our plane would leave later tonight. "I have some calls I need to make. Get yourself ready to go before eight P.M. I packed my things and met with Dante. I told him what was happening; I also told him to hold down the fort while I was gone. Soon enough, the time came when Gerard, Sara, and I got on the plane to head to Base thirty-two. The plane ride was only a couple of hours, so once we got off, it was still night.

Sara and I went to the mess hall to talk and get some late-night snacks. I asked her what kind of mission she had. She said her mission was classified even to me.

She didn't know which city she would be going to, but she did know that they needed her Plant Magic to help grow food.

"That's about as much as I can tell you," she shrugged.

I nodded. "It must be important." After we ate, we called it a night and headed off to bed; Sara had to wake up early for her mission.

The next morning, I noticed Sara had already left to start her new mission. I took my time touring around the base, watching the men train.

I was told to lay low, so I spent the next few days working on my physical strength. I often thought of Sara, Dante, and the rest of my men. One day, while, I was exercising, Gerard approached me. He had a serious look on his face, he handed me an envelope.

"A mission?" I opened it up and saw the mission was a T4 S rank. "I don't do elimination missions," Gerard told me to keep reading. I continued to read until my eyes froze on one sentence.

The mission was to kill The Necromancer that was hiding out at Breon. My hands trembled; my anger got the better of me. All those feelings of hate and sorrow that pained my heart were now focused on a single target. "I'll do it."

Chapter 10: Final Mission

Gerard left me a file with my mission information inside. I looked at photos of the necromancer, his height, weight, and a list of his various magic abilities.

Necromancy was at the top of the list of his powers; however, there was no data on how many people he could summon or how long he could summon them.

I wondered... if he could force me to fight Dylan. His second ability was an energy shield that he could create quickly.

His third ability was teleportation by eyesight, which he had learned from a man who has eluded the INM still to this day. I read a note at the bottom that said you cannot sense his mana or hear him.

I turned the page to see what weapons he used, but that information was limited. Reports from run-ins with him have said he could create energy-based weapons out of thin air.

I decided to take a look at the map of the city. I looked at the geographical layout of Breon and saw an open field next to it. This was the spot where we would have our battle. Somehow, I'll have to lure him there.

I messaged Gerard, "If there was a way that a spy could have the Necromancer unknowingly come to me." Gerard told me he had quite a few spies in Breon and said to me that it was doable. Once I get the Necromancer out into the open, I need to block his vision so that he can't escape. I told Gerard I would hide in a nearby forest just beyond the field.

I will wait there in meditation until the necromancer comes to me. My plan was clear and set. I made my way to the forest by the open field and began to connect to the environment.

I relaxed myself and began to focus on the elements. I began to use the elements as my senses. I started to manipulate the wind and earth to feel what was around me.

My eagerness was making me impatient. Suddenly, I felt something. My Earth Magic could sense the footsteps of someone walking toward the field. I created a slight breeze and swept it past him. In my mind's eye, I could see his face through the wind. I had a feeling this could be him... the Necromancer.

I could feel little pockets of warm air moving around at the edge of the field. I created a heavy fog, placing it near the far edge of the city. Using my Wind Magic, I pushed the fog behind him and blocked his view of Breon. The reports were correct, I couldn't sense his mana at all. I started to gather the surrounding clouds to prepare for battle.

It's time... I walked out into the clearing; he spotted me but made no effort to move or escape. Once I got closer, I looked at the picture to confirm that this was him. He looked at me briefly and looked away. He took a deep breath and then turned his attention back to me. He sent a pulse wave; I assumed he wanted to see how powerful I was.

I took this opportunity to intensify my mana and show my true potential. I went into my empowered form to show him that I meant business.

I wanted him to know what he was going to be up against. Yet I noticed that he was calm, almost like this was rehearsed. I squinted and noticed something coming out of his hand. It seemed like some sort of a bow. He fired energy bolts from it.

Dante's electric enhancement significantly improved my reflexes. I created an earth wall and, at the same time, lowered the earth below me. I wanted to see if the energy bolts could make it through my earth shield. My earth wall intercepted two out of three bolts that clashed with it, but one successfully penetrated the exact spot where I was standing. It was eerie, it's not that I couldn't hear him, but he was soundless. I noticed that those energy bolts had no sound at all. It felt like I was fighting a ghost.

I could feel a warm air pocket behind me. He teleports that fast? Thanks to my enhanced reflexes, my body had already started to turn and shoot a large fire breath at him.

I jumped up and flew into the sky to get a birdseye view. I saw that the Necromancer was encased in this orange-yellow energy sphere.

It had protected him from my fire blast. I quickly shot lightning tendrils from my fingertips, but they barely scratched the shield. I intensified the lightning branches into a single lightning stream. I saw that his shield had begun to crack and in that moment, I looked up to smile at him. But he was gone; the shield that protected him was still there, but he wasn't inside. Then, the color of the shield began to change; I created an earth wall between me and the shield. The earth wall was destroyed by the explosion.

I didn't see anywhere in the report that he could detonate the shields. The moment I recovered from the blast, I saw energy bolts fly past my head. I dodged and created more fog so the advantage would return to me.

I could sense where he was in the fog. His teleportation was too fast. I needed to slow him down. I continued strengthening the sky above, thinking I might need more power.

His energy shield is a strong defense; I would need something with a little more power. I tried to shoot a more intense fire breath to see if it could break through his shield. Finally, I made some progress; his shield was scorched and started to deteriorate, but he could still slip out. He tried to hide in the fog; I took this opportunity to shoot another large fire breath. Which clashed with another shield of his, but his shield faltered this time. He detonated this energy shield as well. The blast pushed the fog out of the way, which worried me. I wanted to give him no advantages.

I filled the gap with more fog. The Necromancer realized that there was no place where he could go to escape me.

I watched him to see what his next move might be. I made the mistake of blinking and in a moment, lost sight of him. Instinctually, I turned around, finding that he had teleported behind me again.

He was standing on some orange-yellow energy platform and started shooting more energy bolts at me from his bow. Tracking him became easier; I could feel his hot body in the cool air. I chased after him shooting empowered lightning bolts at him. Finally, some of my lightning bolts started to pierce through his shield. It wasn't enough to reach him, however. The Necromancer looked at the scale of the storm and at me with wonder and curiosity. He didn't seem scared or worried at all.

I began to charge the clouds, preparing one of my strongest attacks. I let the clouds rain down upon us. It worked; I slowed down his movements, and more of my lightning bolts started to make contact with his energy shields.

Our battle seemed endless, yet It felt like I wasn't fighting anyone. He hadn't even said a single word; every attack he threw at me was soundless. As I was in pursuit, he suddenly just disappeared. I found him quickly, he was standing on the ground.

He just decided to stop fighting. I used this to my advantage, gathered all the electrical energy from the storm, and shaped it into a lightning javelin more powerful and potent than the one I created during my second aptitude test. This was without a doubt, the strongest lightning attack I had ever conjured. I couldn't hold it directly. Small branches of electricity held it inches away from my hand. I aimed and prepared my attack.

The Necromancer seemed distracted. I stopped the rain to see what he was doing. The Necromancer reached out with one hand and opened some incredibly bright portal.

I couldn't hear what he said, but I knew he was talking to someone. Whatever he was doing, I couldn't let this opportunity pass.

"This is it! It's now or never!"

I couldn't let him summon reinforcements, I saw that his hand was reaching out to touch the portal. I used all my remaining mana and fired my lightning javelin, a bright light came from the Necromancer's position.

In a moment, there was a blinding explosion. My lightning javelin had collided with something. The shock wave was so intense that it threw me back toward the city of Breon. I had enough mana to create an earth hill to soften my landing. I was proud of how destructive my lightning javelin had become.

I smirked, waiting for the debris to settle. Then I saw him... It was hard to explain, but he physically looked different, younger even. He was inside a three-layered energy shield.

My javelin had made it passed the first part of his shield. It even pierced the second layer but not the third. My storm had died out, and the sun broke through the cloud banks. He teleported right before me; I assumed he would finish me off. When I looked at his face, he didn't seem mad or upset.

The Necromancer placed his hand on my head. Images and sounds flooded my mind. I was frozen, just trying to process it all. The Necromancer started to talk to me.

"You're quite an interesting man, Ben. I don't hate you. In fact, I understand why you see me as your enemy. Unfortunately, you know nothing about me.

"I have questions that need to be answered." The Necromancer then raised his hand and opened a different kind of portal than the one I saw earlier. He turned back to me and, smiled, and walked into the portal. In a single moment, he was gone. I sat there in silence. My mind had just received a lifetime of memories and experiences.

Once I was able to move, I dragged my body to the edge of Breon and saw Light. I was confused and exhausted, but I recognized Light immediately. I was almost relieved to see him. I excitedly went to greet him. "Hey, Light!" Light teleported in front of me and knocked me out with a punch. When I woke up, I was in a jail cell with my hands tied behind my back. Light was sitting in a chair. It looked like he was waiting for me to wake up. As soon as he noticed I was awake, he started to demand answers.

Where is Aaron? My mind was still numb, and my head hurt. He went into a dimensional portal of some kind.

Light was upset. "Was that you who made the storm?"

I gave Light a tired "Ya." Light studied me. So you're the wolf of Covenhiem Benjamin Cardovic.

I couldn't help but think that Light was my friend. Even though I never met him before. I asked, "Why do I see you as my friend?" Light tilted his head. Aaron could see other people's memories and give his own. His words made sense to me, and I began to understand what was happening to me. Light was conflicted with what to do with me. Light walked closer to the cell and asked, When will Aaron return? I still had trouble thinking straight and told him I didn't know. Light was frustrated and remarked, "I'm well aware know you can escape anytime. Just know I could end your life in the blink of an eye. Light walked out and left me alone.

Now that I was left with my thoughts, I could see Aaron's memories more clearly now that I was alone. I wanted to understand my enemy, so I looked back. I was trying to figure out what kind of man Aaron was. The more I looked, the more I realized he was not the man I thought he was. I didn't appreciate being confined in a concrete cell. After two days, I couldn't take it anymore.

I freed myself to look around; as I walked out, I noticed it was night. Light teleported in front of me the instant I stepped outside. "Where do you think you're going?" Light questioned. I didn't raise my mana or try to make any sudden movements. I told Light, "I wanted to go for a walk." I told Light, "I don't intend to do any harm or cause any trouble. If I do, feel free to kill me."

Light stared at me cautiously, "I'll hold you to your word."

After saying that, Light turned into a light beam and teleported away. I began walking around the city; things looked so familiar to me, yet I had never been here before.

I walked past a small home at the end of a street market. It was the only home on this block with its lights off. I knew who had lived here. I could feel tears running down my face. I had to walk away from that house; I was, overwhelmed with grief.

I could feel Light's eyes watching me. The night was getting colder, and I didn't want to raise my body temp for fear Light would attack me.

I headed back to my cell to get some more rest. When I woke up, it was about noon. I wanted to see the city during the day. Light teleported before me as I stepped out again.

He said nothing, but I knew what his presence meant. If I step out of line, it could mean death. I smiled at him and went on wandering the streets. I heard a voice calling my name, but I didn't think someone was actually addressing me. I didn't know anyone in this city. But the voice sounded too familiar, I turned around and saw Sara. She was holding a basket of apples and oranges. Ben! I knew it was you. She reached out and held me in her arms. She sensed that my energy was really low. She looked at me, concerned, and she asked, "What happened?" I kissed her and held her tightly and responded, "I lost." curious, I asked, "So this is the city Gerard sent you to?" Sara responded quickly, "The INM had the government deactivate the Currency ID cards of any mage that opposed the INM. This whole city is made up of people the INM is after. They need food but have no money, so I was sent here to help."

I had been confused about who I was for days, and seeing Sara again helped me remember who I was. Sara asked me if I had reported to the INM yet. I told her, "I didn't have the chance. I'm being watched by Light."

Sara told me she couldn't be compromised and had to return to her mission. Now, I was stuck with two sets of memories and had my own questions to ask.

My mana was slowly recovering, and my body had begun to heal. I walked to the city's edge where I had fought the Necromancer Aaron.

I walked to a dirt hill I created overlooking the battlefield and wondered how our world got to this point. I stopped showing my memories to Alex.

I was deep in thought when you found me here, Alex. I looked over to check if Alex was okay. His eyes were red and puffy. It seemed like he had been crying for a while now. I gave him some space and let him rest for a minute. Once Alex calmed down, he looked at his hands and the battlefield.

"It feels like I did this..." I felt terrible. The memories one receives can mess with your head for a bit.

"Ben, I don't think you're a bad person. I understand the choices you made, and I know your pain. You asked me if anything was out of place or that seemed off. There were a couple of things. One was that my grandpa has been getting younger. The other was the stuff both Quinn and Kash said. Ben, something is off, but I have no clue what it is. I can't put my finger on it." I couldn't help but agree with Alex. But I'm back at square one.

Alex stood up and stared at me with a smile on his face. It lasted a little more than a moment, a behavior reminiscent of his father, Aaron. It almost seemed as if he was savoring the moment.

Alex took a deep breath and announced, "I'm ready. Show me my father's memories." I shook my head in disbelief. "You should wait, Alex. I just gave you a lifetime of memories, and your mind is still processing the ones I gave you. The truth was Aaron's life held more pain and loss than anything I could have imagined. I did make a promise, though... "Alex, you're going to want to sit down for this." I placed my hand on his head, "I will show you the kind of person your father was."

Are you ready for what's to come?